# The Indian Who Bombed Berlin and Other Stories

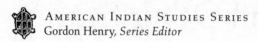

AMERICAN INDIAN STUDIES SERIES
Gordon Henry, *Series Editor*

# The Indian Who Bombed Berlin and Other Stories

*Ralph Salisbury*

MICHIGAN STATE UNIVERSITY PRESS · *East Lansing*

♾ The paper used in this publication meets the minimum requirements of ANSI/NISO Z39.48-1992 (R 1997) (Permanence of Paper).

 Michigan State University Press
East Lansing, Michigan 48823-5245

Printed and bound in the United States of America.

17   16   15   14   13   12   11   10   09      1   2   3   4   5   6   7   8   9   10

LIBRARY OF CONGRESS CATALOGING-IN-PUBLICATION DATA
Salisbury, Ralph J.
The Indian who bombed Berlin and other stories / Ralph Salisbury.
p. cm. — (American Indian studies series)
ISBN: 978-0-87013-847-8 (pbk. : alk. paper)
1. Indians of North America—Fiction. 2. Racially mixed people—Fiction. 3. War and society—Fiction.
I. Title.
PS3569.A4597 I53  2008
813'.54 22—dc 21
2008038137

Cover design by David Drummond, Salamandar Hill Designs
Book deisgn by Charlie Sharp, Sharp Des!gns

§ green Michigan State University Press is a member of the Green Press Initiative and is committed
  press to developing and encouraging ecologically responsible publishing practices. For more
information about the Green Press Initiative and the use of recycled paper in book publishing, please visit
*www.greenpressinitiative.org.*

Visit Michigan State University Press on the World Wide Web at: *www.msupress.msu.edu*

# CONTENTS

*Part Three.* ALL IN THE FAMILY: SOME VANISHING AMERICAN MILITARY HISTORIES

*Part Four.* TERRORISM AND TERRORIZED

PART ONE

# Coming to Manhood: Some Initiations

# White Snakes and Red, and Stars, Fallen

Boots—Cherokee forebears' moccasins; school-bell—English forebears' summons to man the stockade. Eight-year-old Seek (short for Sikwaya) Ross was daydreaming tomahawks and muskets when, living their own ancestral dream, three dogs sounded wolf cries and bounded down a hillside's drifted snow.

Seek ran, sobbing, "Mith Smi-ith, Mith Smi-ith," wind chilling his tongue, while the thud of paws and the click of toenails against frozen gravel drew closer, and fierce baying grew louder with expectation of the kill.

Then, horn sounding "Be-eep, Bee-eep," a red truck hurtled over the icy crest ahead, skidding without slowing down.

It was on its way to pick up milk cans, which Seek's big brother had helped their father drag out to the gate—but warned not ever, *ever* to take rides, Seek clutched burdock stalks at the edge of the road, burrs biting through mittens, while his hope of rescue sped past, horn sounding "Beepbeepbeep—be-eep," the driver's boyhood's World War Two code "V" for "victory," Seek's skin a reminder of Japanese.

The milk hauler would savor—and share with other men drinking beer—memory of white and red stripes stretched across "pretty tits" while the teacher'd struggled to tether Old Glory against wind. His appreciative "Be-eep, Be-eep" offered or inflicted, like his and his army buddies' girl-chasing "wolf-whistles," he'd sped on, past a little Indian standing in roadside snow and "three scruffy mutts vamoosing faster'n greased lightning" as the truck horn's victory "V" resounded off surrounding trees.

Flag stripes, white snakes and red, coiling and striking in wind, Seek stumbled into line, too breathless to parrot the Pledge of Allegiance his teacher was reciting, her lipsticked lips as red as flag stripes, teeth white between, her white-gloved left hand jerking her wind-blown blue dress hem down over a glimpse of nylon, shiny like ice at the base of the flagpole, her right hand a five-pointed pale star, flared against the swell of her dark blue coat.

Above the flag, bombers, as shiny as attendance-roll stars, drew white stripes across blue, as they did every day, to warn, to intimidate, and to protect.

"Wild dogs, my foot! Wild imagination!" Seek's golden-haired goddess decreed, and her gemmed hand flashed down roll call—a meteor, cataclysmic, striking her tardy little worshiper's star from the gold perfect-attendance constellation.

"I don't want to hear it, don't want to hear it," Miss Smith had to say, say, say again and again and again, every day, every single day, voice like Seek's mom's calling her children indoors, neither Seek nor his big brother allowed out to play until the brood mare's mating-whinny no longer sounded as loud as a TV scream, and the stud was again in its owner's trailer, big black butt and red-ribbon-tied tail again robed in road dust.

Before she'd be "back from the backwoods," back in her home city, back in the twentieth century, Miss Smith would have to endure months of hearing whining about who cussed who, who shoved who, and who bloodied whose nose.

Big kids forever, forever deviling small, it was natural to guess that the all-boy big brother—absent today—had seized on his younger sibling's fear of walking to school alone and had started the little bookworm daydreamer's wild Indian imaginings about wild dogs, with bodies so bristly with brown burdock burrs they'd looked "as big as bears."

Desperate, Seek mumbled a plea—as hopeless as his whimpered "Mith Smi-ith, Mith Smi-ith," or the would-be-lover, milk-truck driver's "Be-eep, Bee-eep"—"Can I—?"

"*May* I," Miss Smith corrected, gold spines around engagement gem prickling like burdock burrs as she gently fisted streaked tears from a high-boned cheek as brown as a grocery bag.

"May I bring my bow and arrow to school tomorrow?"

Gem-finger thunderbolt aimed at black eyes gazing beseechingly up, the goddess demanded, "What for? To shoot another girl? *Or me?*"

Remembering his arrow flown crooked in wind, feathers crimson against snow, just before black tip struck white stocking, Seek cried, lapsing into the lisp he'd all but outgrown, "Oh, Mith Smith, I'd never—*do tha-at* to you," mumbling *"do tha-at"* because he couldn't bear to repeat "shoot" after hearing Miss Smith say it, her voice breaking as his mother's did, praying over his sister's name on a little stone in a row with big stones.

Hauling flapping flag down from its rickety wooden pole—the last of duties, which ranged from bandaging cuts to scrubbing little kids' malnutrition-thin poo-poo off board seats of hole-in-the-ground toilets—motherly Miss Smith, soon to be a Mrs., saw her "little Indian" hiding behind the schoolhouse and, worried that his parents might worry, drove him home.

White and really quite nice, and no doubt trying to do the best she could under the circumstances, the mother drew back from a window, and dimly visible through frost, whipped off her apron, smoothing glowing, graying, blond hair.

Afraid that her wild Indian pupil's wild Indian father would be home, Miss Smith braked short of snow-topped gate posts.

Enduring and even artfully encouraging some middle-aged hillbilly versions of flirtation, she had eloquently, passionately pleaded for a new, rust-proof flagpole, whose shining height would be worthy of Old Glory and show that all she'd endured in this cultural badlands had been for the nation defended by her dad, killed while invading Algeria. But the Ross boys' crude, half-breed-Indian father had persuaded an all-too-ready-to-be-stingy school board that the pole would be "as useless as tits on a boar."

Opening the car door into nostril-shriveling cold, Seek's pretty teacher glanced toward her pupil's mother's kitchen window and laughed. "You see, Seekie, except for your neighbor's big white dog, chasing my car going past, we saw nothing—nothing at all."

"Theekie thaw wild dogth big ath bearth," big boys taunted next day, after Pledge of Allegiance, "but dogth didn' EE-EAT Theekie, dogth thinkth Theekie'd tathe't yukky."

The teacher thought a little teasing might teach the little day-dreaming tyke that his made-up stories were what most called, with more rhythm than originality, "big fat fibs." However, Seek's brother, who was twelve and very manly, presented the parental excuse for yesterday's absence, and while his rough fingers boldly lingered in his pretty teacher's palm's smooth warmth, he told her that dog tracks led almost to where he'd found Seek's mitten snagged on a burdock bush. Eyes as blue as his blond mother's, under black bangs, the older brother looked white and did not tell fibs. He'd knocked flat a bigger boy, angrily explaining, "He gived me the lie"—voice virile and quite frightening, like his dad's.

"WooWooWoo! WooWooWoo! Oh, Mith Thmith, Theekie'd never do THA-AT to you-oo—never never do tha-at to you-oo-oo."

"I'm sick of this backwoods school," Miss Smith cried, red-lipsticked lips parting, revealing moist, pink, secret inner mouth. "Dads giving boys smutty magazines and shooting each other in taverns. More janitoring than teaching."

Big for his age and "better brought up" than most, Seek's brother always helped her carry coal from the woodshed.

"Smelly outdoor toilets." She stopped—didn't want, want to have said it—and of all things, to a pupil obviously a little sweet on her, a kid who'd never hung his young bohunkus over anything more modern than a hole in the ground.

"Dogcatcher I'm not," she sobbed behind the folded flag. "Have your wild Indian father phone the law."

Propping his ax against the chopping block and brushing back gray ghosts of his wedding photo's black, Indian-style bangs, the boys' dad squinted into his hat and repeated, "Law?" as if reading the stained sweatband's trademark—"& Sons" its surviving gilt.

The youngest was always making up some wild tale, but the older had seen tracks of dogs, stretched wide, running full tilt to jump a fence into the road, then running back into the woods so's not to get hit by that speed demon going like a bat out of hell in his milk truck.

Reckless drivers, young punks taking advantage of a farmer's wife home alone, grown men monkeying around with little girls, *and* for Christsake *boys*—if it wasn't one damned thing to worry about, it was another; but you had to grit your teeth and send your kids to school, like the law said. So, what was a man supposed to do?

"You can take my pistol," he decided. Then—seeing his eldest son grinning, tickled pink, a chip off the old block, absolutely, but maybe a little too cocky for his own good—"Hide it under your shirt so's not to get your teacher all exercised. When they's a bunch of dogs gone to the bad, they's always others will follow, and last week, the milk hauler he had to give our goofy neighbor's dog the damned good butt-kicking it's been a needing since't it was a pup. Don't go shooting that white mutt just for barking its damned fool head off when you pass, but if it comes at you, make sure it don't come but the once't."

The milk-truck driver could not identify any customers' dogs gone wild, but they'd been on farms, everyone guessed, trained to chase thieves from gasoline barrel and foxes from chicken coop, each as protective of its master's children as if they had been its own pups.

Then—a surge of Arctic wind baring curved fang moon, a shift in sunspots, the urging of the devil—for miles around, howls yearned toward sky's glittering-eyed packs. There was a lot of local theorizing, and agreement that you couldn't keep a watchdog tied up, like the law said, no matter what.

"You can sneak your bow and arrow past Mom and hide it just before we get to school," Seek's big brother whispered, afraid, even though he had a gun. "I'll shoot fast and kill the two biggest dogs when they come closing in on us, like they did on you. Aim at the smallest, pull that bowstring back past your ear, and make damned sure you shoot straighter than you did when you aimed at a tree and hit a girl."

"No need for any bow and arrow!" the goofy old bachelor neighbor yelled. "All Whitey's done is yip at you a little bit for walking too close past my gate."

Seek's brother started to reassure the old man—"The bow and arrow ain't because of Whitey"—but hearing its name, in a stranger's voice, the dog crouched to spring. Clutching his bow in one hand, arrow and lunch sack in the other, Seek ran for school, turning his head enough to find his brother backing after him, eyes on the snarling dog, hand on gun inside jacket.

In fresh snow on the same stretch of road where Seek had been chased, they saw paw prints and the bloody fur of a recently killed rabbit, but they did not see the three wild dogs, and they heard only the crackle of ice under their boots.

A little girl from Seek's arithmetic class failed to answer roll call. Miss Smith called the name a second time. Then, calling the name of the little girl's older sister and hearing only silence, she removed two gold stars.

After answering a knock on the schoolhouse door later that morning, she demanded: "Mr. Ross," calling Seek's brother what storekeepers called their father, "pull up your shirt and show me what that bulge is all about."

Hearing "bulge," big boys snickered, and sapphire-flashing fingers flinching back from her "pet pupil's" hand, Miss Smith pointed at the broom closet, for the pistol to be withdrawn from Seek's big brother's waistband and put atop a stack of impounded magazines that big boys had borrowed from fathers to show big girls photos of men and women "as bare-assed as baby birds."

On the way home from school, Seek's brother realized that the white dog's owner had wondered why only the younger boy carried a weapon, and had told Miss Smith about the older boy's thrusting a hand inside his jacket.

"In case those wild dogs come after us or that damned white dog, I'd better be the one to do the shooting," Seek's brother said, lifting Seek's bow and arrows from the weeds where Seek had hidden them. Then he added, words startlingly polite, "if it's OK with you."

His brother killed in the Korean War a few years later, Seek would remember "if it's OK with you," and his response, "Sure, you can use my bow and arrow"—the exchange as close as he and his brother would ever come to saying, "I love you."

Ice-crusted snow crackling like glass, a white blur hurtled from the neighbor's lane, slammed Seek down, and tore at his arms, instinctively clamped to his throat.

Through the intermingled clouds of his own breath and raw-meat-smelling breath, Seek saw his brother's black arrow tip, aimed where faintly shadowed white fur showed space between ribs; but the old bachelor neighbor rushed from his house, bareheaded and coatless, screaming, "Don't shoot!" and, Seek's mitten still snagged on teeth, the dog whirled toward its master's voice, Seek's brother's arrow burying itself almost to its crimson feathers in snow.

His white pet crouched between white boot socks, the old man mumbled, breath cloud a wispy gray beard against brown shirt, "Next time, see you keep away from my gate."

Another arrow nocked, but polite to any grownup, as he'd been taught, Seek's brother replied, "Yes, sir."

"Please don't take Dad's pistol to the sheriff" was all he'd said as Miss Smith's closet padlock had clicked.

"Get inside before you freeze," Seek's mom scolded, her own body shivering, loose apron's blossoms trembling like wind-disturbed real roses, and she shoved her sons back into the door—which their dad, one hand finding glittering truck key, other gripping shotgun, had left open to blown snow.

Hastily unfastening jingling buckles, Seek and his brother removed snowy boots on the storm porch and rushed into the house in time to hear, through sunset-crimsoned storm windows' thick frost, what sounded like distant summer thunder.

Hours later, a TV gunshot reminding him, Seek whispered, "Do you think Dad's in Dutch?" But his brother only pointed at the show they were getting to watch past bedtime. Across the room, their mom's head was bowed as if at prayer, tears reflecting green radio-dial glow.

Cowboys were shooting and Indians were falling off horses, but when headlights flared into the snowy driveway, Seek ran and, with his thumbnail, scraped a peephole in frost. He feared that someone was coming to say that his father was in jail, but it was the family pickup truck which threw back a glittering torrent from spinning tires and skidded to stop, brake lights crimsoning ice.

Stamping oblongs of snow onto the black doormat and leaning his shotgun against a chair, Seek's dad said, "That white dog, he learned too late not to go after no son of mine. And that pretty little young schoolmarm we hired, I don't know what she expects the pupils to learn from her. First, she wants to tax extra for that flagpole, as useless as—" Seeing the boys' mother's hand jerk up from a pan as if burned, he stopped. Then, he took his pistol from his coat pocket and muttered, "Just like one of them comm-you-nists on TV, she tries to get the sheriff to con-confist-ticate a family man's protection weapon instead of going after them sex-maniac drug addicts, and them gas thieves, and those Chicago ma-free-ohsos what robs these local banks, not to mention the . . . the gosh-darned banks themselves, what charges all that interest and all them so-called sirr-vice-charges, taking a man's money he worked his . . . tail near off to earn, worse crooks than all the others put together."

Seek—years from reading that the right to bear arms for self-defense had been again and again regained from chieftains, nobles, capitalists, and protection racketeers—felt shame that his dad had gone, in dirty chore clothes, and made pretty Miss Smith come all the way from the bedroom she rented in town and made her open the closet, where the black pistol lay, its thin gun oil smudging big boys' confisticated magazine women in underwear as vivid as wedding or funeral petals.

"Yeah, that young, stuck-up, know-it-all schoolmarm she'd heard the same radio news, and she was crying and telling me she hadn't took the danger serious and felt like she'd killed the little girl herself," Seek's dad told Seek's mom, who whispered, "Don't tell the boys. They need sleep."

It seemed she meant they'd have to wait till tomorrow to find out about a long cardboard box that their dad had leaned beside his shotgun; but, wrapping tape spiraling down from their dad's blade, a carbine emerged into lamplight, blue-black barrel gleaming like those drawn from cavalry scabbards, to kill tonight's TV Indians.

"Them three wild dogs, they run like greased lightning, the milk-truck man said, but no damned dog alive is as fast as high-power bullets."

"Too late," Seek's mother cried. She put one trembling hand on Seek's head, the other hand clenched, as if she were going to hit his father for saying "damned"; but it was her apron-covered breast she struck, flour flying, like a puff of snow, out of blue blossoms. "Too late for the little girl"—and, his parents whispering, going into their bedroom, Seek heard the names Miss Smith had called twice at roll call, before removing two gold attendance-stars.

As they were being driven to school, Seek and his brother saw ruts the pickup truck's wheels had gouged down to clean, white snow when Seek's dad had braked hard in front of the goofy old neighbor's gate. Dawn-shadowed paw prints crossed white yard, the space between prints widening, nearing the road, the dog getting up speed for its leap. Thrown back by shotgun pellets, it had left a crimson snow-angel shape, beside which the old bachelor's knees had made deep hollows. There were two lines of blurry boot prints, those going back to the house deeper from carrying a weight.

Because ice had broken telephone lines, only parents who'd heard the radio news had driven children to school, but so many cars came at day's end, it seemed like the Christmas Program.

In their own truck, Seek and his brother saw the sheep they'd saved by bottle-feeding her when she was a sickly lamb.

"Bait," their dad said, "same way we used to get lamb-killing panthers when I was a boy."

"Could I take the shotgun?" Seek's brother asked, blue eyes searching snowy trees both sides of the snowy road, and their father, brown eyes intent on steering in icy ruts, grinned, "Sure."

Seek saw, faintly reflected in windshield, his own dark eyes gazing beseechingly up through tangles of black hair as he asked, "Could I, maybe, take my bow and arrow?"

His dad only laughed. "And buy another girl new stockings?"

"Tonight, you're the man of the house, Seekie," Seek's mother said, handing him a last dish to be dried, her warm, wet hand patting the cheek of her "sensitive, bookworm, daydreaming" child. The dogs' killing a little girl reminded her that she'd had, for only a few years, a little girl of her own, and she let Seek watch a TV show, with a woman as pretty as Miss Smith giving money to giggling men and women while an audience clapped like parents whose kids had said pieces at Thanksgiving.

Hearing "Bedtime, Seekie," Seek roused just enough to grope, leaning first against his soft, warm mother, then against the chill wall, up the stairs.

Next waking, hearing his brother's snoring on the other side of the bed, he put his bare feet down on cold floor, stumbled to the window, breathed a hole in ice, looked down, and in the gray light of just before dawn he saw the truck, parked as usual beside the porch to keep thieves from siphoning its gas.

One hand gripping an ear so thick with brown burdock burrs it looked like a bear's ear, Seek's dad was dragging a dog from the truck, and a bigger dog was already sprawled in snow, one eye glittering between clinched burdock burrs, a crimson halo circling teeth gaped wide between twisted black lips.

His brother still snoring, Seek pulled on shirt and pants, rushed downstairs, got into socks, boots, coat and cap, then ran out into the cold, to be alone with his dad and hear about the hunt he'd not been allowed to join.

"When she drives past these fices nailed up and not never going to go after any little girls no more, I reckon your teacher will change her tune about guns and Indians," Miss Smith's "Wild Indian" pupil's dad said, frosty breath turning his black-whiskered lips as gray as the bristly muzzle of the biggest dog.

"You sure are a good shot, Dad," Seek said, as near as he could come to "I love you"—words he'd only heard said mockingly, big boys teasing girls after school.

"Hunting, and then the war—it use't to it was I could shoot, but my eyes is starting to go kaflooey, and that least dog, it got away," Seek's dad said, knuckles lightly tapping his least son's shoulder.

Proud to be helping, Seek hugged the biggest dog's frozen corpse against the gate post, and as his dad hammered a spike between yellow fangs, blood oozed from shotgun-pellet wounds and, frozen, was jolted into a red sleet, which stung Seek's face.

The two bigger killer dogs dead, the least one would have gone back to being its master's herd dog, guard dog, and friend, Seek's dad had said; but, Seek's brother staying home and sleeping, Seek ran between ranks of skeleton trees, loose boots slipping in truck ruts—ran, panting cold air between aching teeth, until he reached school.

For the five days that constituted a school week, the flag was only raised to half-mast.

Right hand bared to the cold, her red nails pressed against blue-sweater swell, a dead war hero's daughter led in pledging allegiance, her lipsticked lips as red as flag stripes, teeth white between, and America's future citizens followed their teacher's example, cold fingers five-pointed stars, raised to heartbeats.

"My next pledge of allegiance will be my wedding vow," Miss Smith had giggled, engagement gem flashing as she'd accepted, from her "wild Indian pupil's" blue-eyed big brother's rough, lingering fingers, the folded flag.

Bombers overhead—flying to warn, to intimidate, and to protect—Seek would watch as the flag from his brother's coffin was folded as small as a blanket wrapped around a new-born baby and placed in their combat-veteran father's trembling hands.

Seek, both a revenge-seeking redskin and a redcoat, summoned to man the stockade, would remember his teacher as he stared at an army swearing-in officer's red-lipsticked lips and white teeth.

Seek became, like millions of others, a soldier, a killer. Then, as docile as a wild dog returning to being a watchdog, he watched over children, his own and those in an Indian school, chapped lips and milk-tooth rows stretching into flag stripes, pledging allegiance every morning of the school week, five days—five fingers lifted to count—five senses drilled into habit—nine months of school leading to graduation—nine months of pregnancy leading to birth—life—death.

# Bathsheba's Bath, Bull Durham Bull, and a Bottle of Old Granddad

"At twelve, Cherokees is men and ought not to devil a child," Lackey York's grandmother had told Lack's cousin Tad, to shame him for teasing Lack, two years ago. Twelve now himself, sparse hair on his chin, Lack was about to start to slowly, slowly learn, and to forget and forget and forget, that manhood means more than having to shave.

Granny's experience of men included her marriage to Lack's father's white father, who'd abandoned her and their three small sons, all of whom she had raised to manhood, only to lose the eldest in the war Lack's father had survived, the War to End All Wars, called—now that another war had begun—World War One. On previous visits, Lack's family had stayed with Granny, but this time they stayed with Lack's father's younger brother, Uncle Clyde. Uncle Clyde was the first Indian to be elected sheriff in Boone County, Kentucky, but he never mentioned his Indian blood. Election photos showed him as the young soldier he'd been twenty-three years before the bombing of Pearl Harbor, his uniform adorned with two medals.

Becoming sheriff—and receiving bribery money from bootleggers—had enabled Uncle Clyde to buy a house, five times the size of Granny's log cabin. In an upstairs room, called the Boys' Room, Tad slept on his own bunk. His little brother and Lack shared a double bed for two nights—and then, after some low-voiced grownup talk downstairs, they were joined by twenty-some-year-old Kenny, the son of the brother who'd been gassed to death, in a battle that Lack's father and Uncle Clyde had survived.

His own war scarcely begun, Kenny had been sent home missing one eye and missing part of his mind. His cancer-afflicted mother's funeral had been held the day before he came home with Uncle Clyde, and his hands—clutching his two paper-bagfuls of possessions—had been shaky, his real eye red and glistening from tears.

"Poor boy, he never had him no daddy, account of the one cussed war, and account of this new cussed war, not never no wife to take his mother's place now that she's gone. All night, he laid by that cold grave, a carryin' on so mournful he set all the hounds to howlin' with him. Oh, how he must of loved that old ma of his," an old woman had rhapsodized over the backyard fence.

"Her son he loved her, and all of us we loved her, with boundless Christian love," Uncle Clyde's wife, Aunt Liz, had replied. Later, she'd sobbed to Lack's mom, "Kenny's mother she suffered. Lord! how she did suffer! And, now, she's found peace—the peace what passeth understanding—she's found peace."

Cousin Tad had seen feathers spiraling above the trash-burning barrel, and he and Lack used sticks to sift charred pillow-case remnants among subsiding flames. Risen from a bullet hole, centering a blood stain, white ashes had swirled away on shrieking wind.

Cousin Kenny worked as a swing-shift guard at a defense-plant gate, and after he came home in the middle of the night, his grief-tormented body ceaselessly creaked bedsprings in the darkness, beyond Lack's six-year-old cousin's soft snores.

Lack's Mom, finding out about the new sleeping arrangement, did not want to say what it wasn't her place to say in another woman's house, but she said anyway, low-voiced, that she was worried her little nephew and her twelve-year-old son might catch the "Bad-Disease" off sheets "profaned" by their bachelor cousin.

Lack's aunt nodded, happy to share in sisterly worry, but she would have to bring the subject up with her man, as she did with everything except what directly concerned God.

At the start of Lack's visit, fourteen-year-old Tad had talked and talked with Lack's fifteen-year-old sister, and he'd ignored Lack as if Lack had not been twelve, and almost thirteen; but after Lack's sister had said something emphatically, and after Lack had shared in finding the bullet-pierced pillowcase in the trash barrel, Tad had started treating Lack as if they were the same age. When he asked his mother if he could take Lack to a film "based on the Bible," his mother decided—for her Baptist self, for her therefore Baptist husband, for Lack's noncommittal dad, and for Lack's Lutheran mom—"Yes."

From the balcony—called "Nigger Heaven," though Lack's was the only even somewhat dark complexion to be seen off-screen—Tad and Lack watched white-diapered men endure being whipped while bucket-brigading donkey milk up steep steps. The men were called slaves, even though they were as light-skinned as Lack's college cousin's books' pictures of Indians captured by Spaniards and put to work.

Enslaved by hormones, Tad and Lack snickered expectantly, with a multitude of males, on hearing that handmaidens, their swirling silks mist in sunset wind, meant to bathe Bathsheba in "the milk of a thousand asses."

Peeping between curtains, an armor-plated Bible-days knight, a sappy expression on his whiskery kisser, sighed, "I've glimpsed heaven," and was axed and dropped, flopping like a beheaded turtle.

Each time the queen raised a naked arm above opaque donkey milk, the only magic wand Lack knew rose against tight pants, but his wish to see the "all" suggested by "bare but for golden crown" was not granted, Bathsheba finishing her bath—and the film—covered by queen-size "silken" towels, and still wearing the headgear said to be of the metal for which Spaniards had invaded The New World.

Trying to enjoy more than he'd understood, Tad ventured that women swirling glowing silks around the beauty of shadowy mysteries were called "handmaidens" because they gave "hand-jobs" to armor-encumbered spearmen. Eunuchs got to see all that there was to see of handmaidens, and even all of the queen—but because their "family jewels" had been cut off, they might as well have been ogling trees.

Recognizing that Tad's inventions were intended to make the Bathsheba film his and his alone, Lack bragged, "I've helped cut the balls off boar hogs, to turn them into shoats," pretending he knew all that there was to know, though his sex education had consisted of his Dad's muttering, "You'll find out soon enough, I reckon." Lack had seen thighs flashing as girls swung on playground swings, and he'd seen a monster bull rear up, bellowing, to straddle forelegs around a heifer's haunches. The only one available to wrap a rough burlap sack around slimy little forelegs tipped by tiny hoofs and pull a stuck calf out of its mother, he knew that storks only brought babies in a book.

From his Mom's embarrassment, he'd guessed that his Cousin Kenny's dreaded disease had to do with the "wetter," and when itchy pimples broke out, Lack bashfully sought medical advice from Tad, who'd told a girl he loved her and "smooched her some" and got her to let him put his newly hairy hand inside her newly purchased bra.

"Yes," Tad snickered, "it's the Bad-Disease, really bad. I told you to stay out of those jimpson weeds." He'd told Lack after Lack had already taken the short cut through them, wondering why Tad went around, and now Lack was wondering, more worried than ever, what jimpson weeds, whatever they were, had to do with "the Bad-Disease," whatever it was, and wondering if maybe he'd caught a double dose, off "profaned" sheets and off crotch-high little white flowers, which looked like the ragweed blossoms back home in Iowa, on the farm, where he wished to gosh he was, in his own bed, with only his brother Pete's snoring to bother him and no itchy disease to not understand and to catch all the same.

"Boy, what you have got there is jiggers—little red bugs that you could maybe almost see if you could get your head down close to peek past your weeny, and if you could see them before they dug down into your skin," Tad giggled, and with the salty bacon grease he'd fetched as an ointment burning to beat hell, Lack understood, too late, the giggle.

Desperate, he let his Mom try rubbing-alcohol, which burned worse than the salt, but, misery somewhat soothed by the cornstarch his aunt supplied (unintentionally humiliating him with, "one of those old remedies, for diaper rash") he was cured. Tad became his pal again by getting his girl to get her friend to let his Yankee cousin feel mysterious soft shapes through thin cotton, and then to peek between tiny white buttons.

Cousin Kenny might or might not have "the Bad-Disease," but "bad company" in the army had "cursed that sweet Christian boy" with an affliction that was, Lack's aunt made quite clear, far worse than any disease. Kenny was possessed by the eighth deadly sin—which God had forgotten to prohibit—liquor. And if Kenny lapsed, he could just go back to sleeping on his poor angel mother's cold grave, if it came to that, but one thing sure, he was not going to set foot in Lack's aunt's house ever again.

The last to wake up one morning after grief-tortured moans had kept him awake for hours, Lack knelt to tuck in invisibly profaned sheets on Kenny's side of the bed and, gingerly tugging suspiciously clean socks from a normally dusty boot, found a bottle labeled "Old Granddad." Dreading more sleepless nights, with dreams of smoke rising from a blood stain and swirling away on shrieking wind, Lack saw his chance to get rid of Kenny, and he left the sock askew so his aunt might detect gleams of glass. Tattling outright would have violated the code he'd learned on school playgrounds, and he said nothing, not even to Tad, who might get in trouble with his mother if he knew and did not tell. Kenny kept his own secret by incessantly sucking "whiskey-killer" cinnamon drops before leaving "The Boys' Room."

Each day, Lack saw that the level of amber had, like thermometer fluid, fallen; but each time it reached zero, it returned to full summer.

One evening, Tad took Lack in the family rowboat a mile up the creek to town, docked before they reached the store where they'd buy milk, and instead found a dimly lit street, from whose well-lighted windows women leaned and showed more than what Lack had glimpsed by tremblingly undoing tiny buttons. When one woman called down, "You're the sheriff's boy, that goes to school with my brother," Tad ran, Lack right at his heels.

Shadows among shadows—FBI agents staked out or gangsters ambushing a rival—Tad and Lack innocently risked Bad-Diseases by sharing cigarette butts men dropped, and they watched fistfights between big miners, or between some big miner and an even bigger, and more soberly effective, tavern bouncer.

Next day, to impress Tad's town-kid friends, who only knew meat from supermarkets, Lack imitated his Dad's castration of herd boars to make them salable as pork. With his jackknife, he cut the coconut-size paper scrotum off an elephant-scale Bull Durham Tobacco billboard bull, despite a scribbled warning, "Anywon anymor tamper this sign will be persecute."

To compete with a Yankee kid's having defied "persecution," Tad and his fellow Kentuckians walked the four-inch-wide sign railing twenty feet above sun-glaring blacktop highway. Autos glittery blurs hurtling below, Lack inched, struggling against acrophobia, eyes blurring with sweat or tears, then, in panicky desperation, lunged, bare feet groping for splintery railing, and reached a handhold, the signboard's far edge—above his head, and bigger than his head, the pawing hoof of a bull, which his knife had diminished to steer.

To train their "lightning reflexes," as they'd seen the Heavy Weight Prize Fight Champion of the World train his, in a film, Tad and Lack caught and crushed flies midair—keeping, without a pencil, a frequently disputed count.

Gunshots just down the highway—Lack's mom's frightened cry, "Boys, get in here," too distant to have to heed—Lack stood on the top porch step and saw one of his uncle's deputies leaning precariously out of a prowl car's side window and shooting at a speeding pickup truck.

Lack's lethal fingers unclenched from a doomed buzzing as a lethal buzz sounded and a bullet ricocheted into wood between his feet and those of Tad—Tad quick to open his jackknife and pry out and flaunt the souvenir.

Another echoing pistol shot came from around a curve in the highway, this shot followed by a louder bang—a bullet blowing out a tire, Lack would learn, and would learn that the driver had crashed into the Bull Durham signpost, to be prosecuted not for tampering with the sign, but for robbing a local bank.

"Just a poor, out-of-work miner who couldn't feed his family, be easy with him, be easy," told Lack why his Uncle Clyde had been elected sheriff.

Lack's Dad's and Uncle Clyde's talk, overheard days later, told Lack why his sleep had not been troubled by tortured moans the previous night.

"Seeing this high school boy who was maybe being a little too enthusiastic in a parking lot, Kenny gave the boy a damned good sheriffing, flashing his gate-guard badge like he was one of my deputies and threatening with his billy club while slapping that little shit's whiskers back into his chin. Then, Kenny done shared a bottle with the girl and kept her in his car all night. Her parents phoned the FBI, and I had to talk a blue streak to keep Kenny out of prison."

Tad and Lack had seen Tad's mother pack Kenny's dusty boots and clean socks into a paper bag and throw his remaining whiskey into the trash-burner barrel. Though already summoned to dinner, the boys probed smoldering crust with twigs, and Lack discovered that the bottle was unbroken, its fall cushioned by half-burned news of yesterday's war and the charred feathers of a deathbed pillow.

Lack had not forgotten salty bacon grease in scratched skin, and as unforgiving as a humiliated nation, he dropped the uncapped bottle while he noisily swallowed a ritualistic mouthful, his ash-tasting sacrament burning like jigger itch all the way down.

# White Ashes, White Moths, White Stones

On the verge of becoming a man, Lack heard his aunt say, "Men!" And Lack's Mom nodding in anticipation, Lack's aunt continued, "I've no doubt the girl was trash, like her mother before her, and deserved just what she got, but just the same, that drunken pup Kenny ought to be jailed."

Lack thought of ghostly white ashes swirling in shrieking wind above the family trash burner. He thought, "a high school girl," and it was a thrilling, terrifying thought. What the girl, her boyfriend, and her parents thought and felt, and what persuasion or intimidation had prevented anyone's pressing charges, he never learned, twelve and not entitled to ask, twelve and only able to dream, not live—twelve and still spectator, not actor.

A high school girl, not much older than the eighth-grade girl with whom Lack was, once a week, setting sail for The New World—though scared he'd fall off earth's edge—a high school girl, Lack thought, fascinated, expectant, and afraid. Next month he'd be in high school. His brother Pete had already been there a year, and Lack's girl cousins sighed that his picture was cute. They were "almost" seventeen and "almost" nineteen—"big girls." Their room, which they shared with Lack's sister, was the "taboo temple" of motion-picture posters, the temple door often open on hot nights, tempting Lack with glimpses of bare skin.

Glancing across the living room and deciding that her son was deep in a book—*The Real Life Adventures of Buffalo Bill*—Lack's Mom whispered emphatically, "That drunken Kenny! All those nights here under the same roof! Weren't you just sick with worry he'd take advantage of your girls?" not mentioning her "girl," who was "as pure as the driven snow" or "boy-crazy," depending on Ann's behavior or on her mother's mood.

"My girls," Lack's aunt rebuked Lack's something-other-than-Baptist mother, "is got Jesus watching over them."

If Christ, nailed to one pink-flower-papered living room wall, was "watching" through the opposite wall, He'd be seeing what Lack was imagining, the younger of his aunt's girls dressed only in splashing bathtub suds.

Bubble-bath-scented, she might be in her Lord's care, but according to her mother, another high school girl "deserved just what she got." What Cousin Kenny might have gotten between midnight and dawn, Lack could only guess from peeks between tiny buttons and delicately stitched buttonholes.

After the usual—to him, boring—Sunday morning service, Lack's big-girl cousins asked his aunt if they might go into the hills that night to worship the Deity who daily watched over them. Glad it was a devotion and not some dance, with whiskey on the premises, Lack's aunt agreed that her daughters could make a pilgrimage up into the dark hills, if they were escorted by their brother.

"Sure thing!" was Tad's response, though Sunday night was coal miners' last chance to live it up before being buried in miles of tunnels for five days, and the last chance for Tad and Lack to puff long cigarette butts while watching fights and glimpsing bare-shouldered, short-skirted women welcoming staggering men.

"You'll see," was Tad's only explanation for his turn toward God, but Lack's "seeing" depended on getting permission. His Mom attended his aunt's church to be polite, but she normally practiced her and her dead first husband's religion, Lutheranism, and didn't overdo it. "One should not scoff at another's faith, no matter how strange," she'd said, but having heard that some local sects got women to roll around on the floor with men, she'd decreed that Lack's sister would stay home.

Not naive enough to risk a second decree by asking his mother anything, Lack asked his dad, "Do you think I should go with my cousins to the Holy Rollers meeting?"

"I hear these is Holy Jumpers, not Holy Rollers," his dad recalled. "Holy Rollers whoop and holler and roll between pews, like old Jacob wrassling that angel in the Bible. But Holy Jumpers whoop and holler and jump up and down or at least bounce to beat hell, claiming they been seized by the Power of the Lord."

Once, to satisfy himself that the Power was not just pretend, he had jumped, he said, full weight, onto a divinely possessed man's toes. "I guess it never proved nothing about the religion," Lack's dad reflected, "and maybe not nothing about the feller, except that I never liked him none and he never had any use for me, neither." The feller had sparred some with Lack's dad until "an eye for an eye and a tooth for a tooth" turned into "turn the other cheek."

"You mean 'turn the other toes,'" Lack scoffed, and pleased with his growing baby boy's complicity in word play, Lack's dad said, his eyes turning onto his and his brother's cars, "Your mom don't have to know nothing till after you're back."

The way to where Holy Jumpers would be trying to find their Way to the Lord proved to be a foot-and-hoof-worn path along a moonlit creek, whose ripples glittered like a Christmas candle procession. In college and, as her Baptist mother put it, "a studying them old fool beliefs what her granny still takes stock in," Lack's eldest cousin intoned—murmured words mingling with the ceaseless murmuring of creek current's surge toward sea—"Hundreds of centuries of rain carved this canyon; and here, a Cherokee medicine man prayed for braves—scalp-locked, red-painted, and stripped for battle." Like Lack, she loved reading, and she had, she said, "taken a shine" to Lack's bashfully pleased, Indian-skinned self. Lack loved her eyes, as dark as his own—loved her voice, which sounded like books and like singing. He loved her with a shy, twelve-year-old's love, different from what he felt about unfastening buttons and fondling.

As Lack and his cousins climbed a dark hill, shadowy forms emerged from side trails. Some were couples, some were women in pairs or in groups, and some were men together, their moonshine whiskey gleaming in moonlight, jugs passing from mouth to mouth, a lot of scoffing passing from mouths to ears. Scoffing spectators and worshipers ascended toward an insistent pealing like that from bells hung around necks of cows, to prevent their being lost.

Meant to serve twenty centuries of Christianity, the church they finally reached was no bigger than the one-room school that Lack had attended for eight years back home, and, like his grandmother's cabin, the church was walled with logs. Stripped of bark, a pale, skeletal, tepee-shape steeple's four poles raised crossed sticks toward sky. The churchyard was a clearing studded by stumps, whose recently sawed tops shone white in the glow of three bonfires—which glowed also in the white hair of a man hugging sisters and shaking brothers' hands at the door. He was tall, pale, and skeletal, like his church's steeple; but when his narrow chest expanded his white shirt out between tight black coat lapels, his voice was louder than his belfry bell, welcoming Lack's "young lady" cousins, who got—Jesus' bare-arm-patting pastor watching over them—the seats of reluctantly yielding men.

Tad then dragged Lack outside to the only window; but, jostled aside by bodies as big as those of miners they'd watched fighting behind taverns, they could only see when the lifting of moon-reflecting jugs to lips left space between armpits and arms. Fueled by "dinosaurs' swill squished into oil" (according to Tad's science teacher), a lantern hung from a nail, dim flame haloing white hair as the preacher began striding back and forth, his hands' shadows big black bat wings fluttering across enraptured faces, across bare arms raised in prayer, and across black dress fronts bouncing to the rhythms of exhortation.

"The Power, Brothers and Sisters, the Power, can you feel the Power, can you feel the Power, can you feel the Pow—er, can you feel it yet, can you feel it yet? Don't hold back, let it, let it, let it take hold, hold, hold of you, the Pow—er, the Pow—er. Can you feel it? Feel it, feel it!"

The deep voice rose and fell, rose and fell, while Lack grew sleepier and sleepier, only rousing when a whiskey jug lifted and he saw, in soft lantern light, a young woman rocking back and forth, back and forth, next to the window, close enough to touch, her pale nails fumbling the front of her black dress—more and more white emerging, bouncing, quivering, becoming the crescents Lack had glimpsed between his awkward fingers while nervously unbuttoning his girlfriend's blouse. The woman was bouncing and bouncing, and the Holy Jumper preacher was chanting and chanting, "The Power, the Pow-er, the Pow—er-er, can you? can you? you can, you can, you can feel it, feel it, feel it, feel it, let it, let it, let it—The Power, the Pow-er!—let it take hold of you, take hold of you, your soul, soul, soul, the Holy Spear-it, the Holy Spear-it, feel it, feel it, feel it, feel it, let it, let it, let it, let it," and within black dress-front's tepee "V," white crescents were growing, growing, glimpsed beneath a big arm lifting whiskey jug to lips, sucking, sucking, sucking, and just when Lack had seen or had almost seen a full moon shape, it was eclipsed by a baby's bald head, bouncing, bouncing, bouncing, and from glittery, asteroid-belt teeth, the moonshine jug plunged, glittering like a meteor, and bounced against Lack's sin-crammed skull.

"The Power, the Pow—er, the Pow—er!" Medicine men chanting and warriors falling and cries rising from dark cabins and beds rocking, back and forth, back and forth—and the "feel, feel, feel," the "let, let, let it," and the screams of joy—and then, big bodies jostled past, and in moonlight, Tad's teeth were flashing as he giggled, "Old fool preacher really had 'em going, really had 'em going, really had 'em going." Tad's giggly chanting sounded scared, and Lack was scared—scared that the only light was one lantern, gone dim, nearly out, in the church—and the light of the moon, when clouds as black as the young woman's dress front let it, let it, let it, and the dark pines' fresh smell and the smell of dinosaurs' swill squished into lantern fuel, and Tad gone into darkness, taking his revenge for the swig of Old Grandad he'd not gotten to take—no sign of the trail down to Lack's aunt's and uncle's house, Lack's mom and his sister, and maybe by now his dad, inside it. Lack's kind, gentle big brother Wulf killing people in unthinkably distant, unreal Europe—and even Lack's big brother Pete and Iowa more miles away than Lack could bear to think, homesick and scared and twelve years old, but feeling as he'd felt as a little boy, trapped between the high, slick clay banks of a creek, and his father's more and more impatient calling finally fading, and the truck motor roaring—then fading into silence.

"Did'ja, did'ja, did'ja feelfeelfeel it?" one of the men with whiskey by his thigh scoffed invitingly to Lack's beautiful college-girl cousin, and "Yes," she answered, seriously, perfectly calm, perfectly polite, "The Power, yes, I felt It"; and "Girl," she said to her bubble-bath-scented younger sister, "I believe our brother is waiting to escort us home."

"And did'ja, let let let it?"

"No," Lack's cousin answered over her shoulder as she left, "I felt It, and then I thought about It too long, and It left me." She left the drunken scoffer to take the drink he'd been offering her, and when he went over backward, as if the invisible fist of God had socked him in the kisser, a friend, guided by bonfire coals glittering in glass, leaped to grab the jug and let its owner go on falling, falling, the thud of his head echoing louder than the pounding of Lack's feet, running after moon glowing off his cousin's, or maybe some stranger's, white Sunday-Best dress.

It vanished, and Lack ran faster and faster, downhill, among dark trees, memory and gravity his only guides, until he heard drunken singing and saw a row of white stones where the path turned. Passing staggering men, he ran, stumbling on the root-ridged path, and heard a girl say something emphatically and slap Tad, who backed up a step, rubbing his cheek.

As Lack slowed to walk beside Tad, the line of snickering men behind them began shouting, "FeelFeelFeel," and pushed a dwarf—no taller than Lack's own five foot one—into the line of women, including Lack's beautiful college-girl cousin and her pretty younger sister, only the Escort, nailed to pink-flower-papered parlor wall, watching over them, from a distance, one of their human escorts snickering in imitation of the drunks, the other human escort scared of being lost, scared of darkness, scared of the drunken men, and scared of the dwarf, whose deranged "Feelfeelfeel" mingled with screams.

"Men!" a woman, whose hair was as white as that of the preacher, pronounced. "Men!" And it sounded like a cuss word.

"Men!" other women repeated.

Urged by indignant wives, two husbands hustled the dwarf back past Tad and Lack, shoved him in among snickering pranksters, then marched just behind the slender silhouettes of girls and women while the single men gradually dispersed onto dark side paths, the last three giggling, "Feelfeelfeel" in farewell when, dragging the grown man of Lack's same size with them, they turned from moonlit creek-bank trail onto highway and lurched toward red roadhouse neon.

Lack's grandmother's "fire-spitting, dragon-monster Uktenas" became headlights plunging past, and shrieking Raven Mocker Witches overhead were the reassuringly familiar nearby airbase's bombers.

Men!

Neither Lack's dad's car nor Uncle Clyde's car was in the driveway.

Men!

Lack and Tad timidly trailed after Tad's sisters toward a brightly lit porch, where their mothers and Lack's "pure as the driven snow" sister sat beneath a glowing cloud as white as a first-communion gown—as white as the nimbuses of angels—white moths winging to immolate themselves and fall, an ankle-high mound of charred bodies slowly mounting toward an unattainably high, glass-enshrined blaze.

# A Volga River and
# a Purple Sea

War three years in his future, his brother and other last year's graduates already enviably headlined as saving French women from Nazis, Cyrus Littlehorse Jones, "the scrappy Arapaho warrior" of local sportswriters' prose, reached, uneventfully, fifteen—male sexual potency's peak, so professors, years in his future, would pontificate—and he lived up or down to his nickname Sy by sighing while daydreaming nightly of slipping sinfully lovely movie temptresses' lingerie's enticingly yielding elastic down cheerleaders' silken, Caucasian skins—then worrying about his mother's noticing while doing laundry.

With all his heart, and with all his hormones certain that he could impress a silver-skated, short-skirted pirouetter on the Aurora, Iowa, ice rink, Sy sped into a figure eight and, halfway through the top half's figure zero, fell.

Still numb to any pains save those of love, he lay, surrounded by gleaming blades, and got numerous glimpses up the thinly stockinged thighs of motherly girls hovering above him. Then, at the clinic, a nurse's blond hair tickled his nostrils and lips as she fluffed pillows.

Encased like a movie mummy from broken ankle to healthy groin, Sy, balancing on crutches, excavated pyramids of books stacked in his brother's closet, and under *American History* found the treasure he'd long sought—his brother's *Spicy Novelette* collection—now Sy's by right of discovery, while German soldiers were teaching his brother European History.

Able to limp by the time municipal skating rink had melted into municipal pool, Sy limbered his stiff ankle by swimming—doctor's orders—among skimpily swimsuited girls. He swam for so many hours, chlorine made his fingers wrinkle like those of old men, who sat on poolside benches, their fondling eyes easing their equivalents of adolescent loneliness.

Day after day, while greedily appreciating whatever images of bare beauty he could ogle without arousing feminine contempt, Sy somewhat improved the awkward dog paddle, which would, in three years, save his life.

"God moves in mysterious ways," the town's preacher had sermoned, and sinful lust apparently forgiven, Sy was tempted to enjoy—with the medical profession's blessing—a month of sloth and recuperation on his two best friends' family's farm, through which flowed a river named Volga, in imitation of the one flowing through America's often-headlined ally against Hitler. For all of June—the month for brides to wave triumphantly from soap-joke-scrawled, tin-can-trailing cars—Sy's friends labored in their father's fields while Sy indulged in reading and rereading the only magazine he'd managed to hide in his suitcase, *Spicy Wild West Tales*—tales about the stripping of doeskin garments from Indian women. Before supper, he and his friends could swim for an hour. Then, after enduring a sermon about a Son ignored six days out of the seven His Father had created, the adolescent trinity could baptize their puberty-bedeviled bodies repeatedly for the remainder of Sunday afternoon.

Sy, the Scrappy Arapaho, and the two Speedy Sioux, Jim and Joe, had been three-fifths of a basketball team's fifty-fifty success until gravity had cut short Sy's prolonging a glimpse of Caucasian inches under a pirouetted red skate-skirt.

Like Sy's much-bullied, black-eyed self, Joe and Jim were taunted as "redskins." The brothers were about as twin as twins could get, and by the time Sy had grown old enough to desire skaters and break his ankle, he and his twin friends had become triplets. Algebra too much for any one of them, the three ganged up on homework, and in after-school battles, they coped with whites' numerical advantage by fighting with six fists or running like hell in three different directions, remaining thereafter submissively peaceful until the next unbearable accumulation of humiliating aggressions necessitated another proud, if finally doomed, Indian uprising.

Girls' sweater swells arousing other uprisings in the struggle for biological survival, Jim, Joe, and Sy did as all boys did—hid what their moms called their "shames" behind algebra, geography, history, or literature books when walking between study hall and classrooms.

Pirouetting skaters, municipal-pool sunbathers, and cartwheeling cheerleaders—then, while doing frantic, ankle-limbering dog-paddling in the brown currents of Iowa's Volga River, Sy could ogle Jim and Joe's skimpily swimsuited nineteen-year-old sister, Jeanine, who was Sy's older brother's sweetheart. From Jeanine, Sy got, for the first time in his life, the chance to learn the difference between love and lust, and he failed that lesson, as he'd failed at exciting ice-skating and at boring algebra.

Because of his broken ankle, Sy had missed his history class's trip to see the heads of Indian-plundering Heads of State, carved into Jim, Joe, and Jeanine's Sioux ancestors' sacred mountain, whose new name mandated the conquerors' mode of life, Rush More. Sy had also missed two weeks of basketball and all of baseball; and he gloomily knew that World War Two would end before he was old enough to shoot rapist-torturer-murderer Nazis and die a hero and have his picture in the paper, as some of his brother's classmates had.

Being dead was an unreal possible minus, but being bored and ignored and totally unimportant was a minus Sy knew better than he'd ever know math. At sex-and-guilt-ridden fifteen, Sy could not foresee Municipal Pool and Volga River's becoming Pacific Ocean. At recklessly courageous not quite sixteen, Sy was unable to foresee a bullet's doing more damage than ice and lechery had done—unable to foresee his being awarded a Purple Heart medal for a wound inflicted not by an enemy, but by a buddy who'd mistaken Sy's Arapaho face for Japanese.

Sy could not foresee short skate skirt's becoming bridal gown. His brother's sweetheart, his friends' sister, Jeanine, the nearest thing to a movie queen he'd seen, he could not foresee that movie images would move him to make the moves that would win him, and then cost him, an enviably blond, hero-worshiping wife, twenty, who at twenty-three would convince a judge that Sy, "an immature and unfaithful mate," no longer deserved her—no way to foresee, no way to foresee.

No way to know that in breaking his ankle bones and thus learning to swim, he'd escape drowning with half of his squad, and instead be able to dog-paddle through blue-as-ink water, turned purple by others' blood, and stumble onto a Philippine beach.

The summer Sy turned a puppy paddle into a dog paddle, capable of keeping him afloat, he could only imagine the breasts that his big brother had almost certainly caressed.

Her lover and protector protecting French women, the poise of nineteen years and a brief swimsuit her only defenses against Sy's eyes, Jeanine did bra-disarranging dives from a flood-felled tree, and glimpses of intimate, untanned skin innocently glistened in the sun of the Month of Brides. Feeling erotic, and also feeling left out because he could not join Jeanine and her two brothers in exciting diving, limp-ankled Sy considered trying a one-footed spring from slippery trunk into brown current surging through submerged branches. Before he could do so or feel cowardly for not doing so, Jim or Joe threw a white rock into calm water and yelled, "Pearl Harbor Pearl Hunt!" The twins swam down, and one surfaced first, pale rock raised in brown hand.

Jeanine breaststroked gracefully, and Sy puppy-paddled manfully around each glittering vortex created by underwater scuffling, and finally Sy frog-paddled, intending to impress, into murky depths, grasped the baseball-size prize glowing like the world's biggest pearl on the mucky bottom, then did a one-pawed dog paddle up—his reward: feminine cheering and teeth gleaming brighter than the Holiest of Holy Grails.

Encouraged by Sy's audacious success, the goddess then joined the boredom-relieving competition, groping slimy riverbed clay, and wrestling her idolater and her brothers, and rising, white stone clutched in fingers clamped between thighs, to claim victory and a share of the world's air.

Sy knew that his feelings for Jeanine were disloyal to her brothers, and to his own brother, but brown water hid his "shame," and made him bold. When tussling amid surging currents slipped swim bra awry on slippery skin, and almost half of two pearls, more precious than Iowa City Art Museum marble, emerged, glistening and lustrous, into sun, Sy—not quite sixteen and afraid he'd lose the only opportunity he would ever have—grabbed for more than stone.

Slapped so hard his cheek tingled as it had when it had struck ice, he tried to pretend he didn't know why.

Instead of slapping him harder for adding hypocrisy to lechery, Jeanine shriveled his miserable, self-besmirched soul with a contemptuous look, then swiftly swam to shore before her unaware brothers surfaced, eager to go on playing their game.

Soon they got bored and resumed daredevil-plunging from the trunk of the drowned tree, leaving their injured pal to dog-paddle alone, feeling sorry for himself and feeling too ashamed to do more than glance at Jeanine, who was absorbed in reading while sunbathing on the family picnic blanket's intricately interwoven bucks and does.

In movies, men who lost sweethearts heroically enlisted to be killed, thus ending the anguish of love denied. Sy limped out onto slippery bark, resolved to redeem himself by diving one-legged and breaking his ankle again and drowning, while life—from wholesome nursing, to sneaky peeping, to shameful groping—flashed before his eyes.

Panicked, he was turning, intending to inch his way back to handholds provided by upthrust roots, when, wet feet slipping, he fell, and, seized by the surging river, was hurtled, floundering, beneath a tangle of submerged branches, frantic struggles only twisting him inextricably.

Breath bubbling from nostrils, exhausted, almost unconscious, he felt an arm clamp about his neck, then felt himself being raised, not from the dead but from near death, toward a glowing surface he had not hoped to gain again. Head wedged between firm biceps and a softness, which he would remember without any tinglings in his "shame," he was towed into the shallows, delivered into the four warm hands of his two friends, and wrapped in an Indian-patterned family picnic blanket.

He felt chastened by the first of what would be several failures to learn that lust isn't love, and he felt more grateful than he'd be again until a buddy—maybe the one who'd mistakenly shot him—braved Japanese bullets, dragged him behind a wrecked tank, and saved him from bleeding to death.

Sy's friend Joe was training at the improbably monikered Fort Bliss when World War Two, the war that followed The War to End All Wars, ended.

In a jungle battle too inconsequential to be named, war had already ended for Sy's friend Jim.

Sy's brother limped home and married his sweetheart in the presence of his family, including one who had betrayed him. Soon, his nation would betray all who had fought for democracy and equality, their Four Freedoms War lost to racism, religious oppression, imperialistic greed, and nuclear-acceleration toward extinction—humans slow, terribly and seemingly fatally slow, to learn.

PART TWO

# SOME STRUGGLES FOR SURVIVAL IN BATTLE, SOME IN BED

# Ival the Terrible,
# the Red Death

"SABER-WIELDING MADMAN BEHEADS FARM DOG" displacing news of Russian atom-bomb threats in his mind, Ival eased the barn door open and, slipping inside, aimed his gun—at swallows startled into flight—at a steel horse-bridle-bit's saber-blade gleam—at a shadow, which became, in light shining through a window's years of spider webs, the gray-haired man Ival had grown up calling "Dad."

"Sam!" he called now, and called a second time, "Sam!" because he wanted to be sure that the sheriff, who was waiting outside the barn, would hear and know that if Sam shot Ival, it would not be because he'd mistaken his stepson for the madman.

Ival's mother had left no will, and Sam had inherited half of the farm, deeded to Ival's real father's Ioway great-grandfather for helping pioneers to dispossess the Sauk Tribe. All of the farm would have been Sam's if Ival had been killed in war, as Sam's own son, Ival's half brother, had been. All of the farm would be Sam's if Ival were killed while helping the sheriff's posse try to recapture the mad killer.

"I searched the barn," Sam told the sheriff, "but my concern is, is he really in the cornfield like you say? or is he going to turn up at my house while I'm gone, and my wife all by her lonesome and pregnant and ain't never shot a gun in her whole life."

Her whole life was maybe thirty years. A year after her first husband had been killed, in the same naval battle which had killed Ival's half brother, Sam had married her—Sam wanting a son to replace the son Ival's mother had given him. If Ival's half brother had lived, Ival would have felt OK about sharing the farm, but remembering drunken whippings he and his half brother had suffered in childhood, and suspecting that his mother had been bullied into not seeing a doctor until it was too late, Ival hated Sam more than he'd ever hated any Nazi.

"If the lunatic comes at you swinging that saber he stole, I know I can count on you, a old marine, Sam," the sheriff said as he let Sam out of the car. "And you, Ival, your army buddies still talk about their sharpshooter Indian sniper, Ival the Terrible, the Red Death."

No—no more killing, Ival thought; but remembering that the mad veteran had been locked up for shooting nine school kids, he let the sheriff drive him to where a road bordered a cornfield that Sam had planted and cultivated while Ival was still in the army. The corn, now as tall as a man, reminded Ival of the Italian vineyard rows he'd skulked through while German soldiers searched for the American sniper, as Veterans Hospital guards were searching for the mad soldier today.

In Ival's telescopic deer-hunting sight, green ears of corn seemed as big as watermelons, and blades, crossing one another, were a blur. If forced to shoot at close range, the crazed man lunging, saber raised, Ival would have to take hasty aim along the rifle barrel; but a crow, perched on a fence post halfway to where the sheriff had placed Sam, was in perfect focus.

Black crow and his stepfather's black hat a confusion, Ival recalled crows feeding on bodies after battles, recalled tattered black robes— frostbitten fingers of Algerian children fumbling to unknot dead soldiers' bootlaces, undo buttons, small fists battling for coats stiffened by frozen blood.

Scope sight aimed where overall straps crossed broad back, Sam would slump against barbed wire. IVAL THE TERRIBLE, THE RED DEATH would headline a news story about one more ex-soldier sent to the Mental Hospital, or hung.

Walking back and forth a long time, looking as far as he could between corn rows, Ival saw a few field mice and some neighbor's cat. Eyes catching a distant movement, he saw—near Sam, whose gaze was turned to the road—a rooster pheasant running, hunkered low, as if fleeing from footsteps too stealthy for Sam's old ears. Ival made sure that his rifle's safety was still on, then aimed at a post near Sam, the telescopic sight showing each filament of moss, as gray as one of the whiskers in Sam's sparse mustache.

A patrol car sped to draw alongside.

"Just practicing my aim," Ival shouted, and the policeman accelerated to keep to his scheduled patrolling.

Leaning his rifle against a fencepost, Sam slipped into the ditch, hastily unbuttoning, no doubt urgent to lose some of the coffee swelling his aging bladder.

The first German Ival had killed had been hunched into bushes beside his truck. "Caught him with his pants down," Ival's sergeant had snickered. "Shoot!"

In trouble if he disobeyed, Ival had steadied his gun barrel against a tree, shifted his aim, slowly shifted it again and again and yet again and waited until the enemy soldier was buttoned up and on his feet.

Sam was looking toward the farmhouse he'd married a half-blood widow to own. Sam's new wife would be working in Ival's mother's kitchen and listening to the radio news, her fear like that of pioneer women working in cabins, husbands plowing land, Indian land.

Sam was still peeing when a huge man, in green army-hospital pajamas, crawled from green weeds and slipped under the cornfield fence. Rising and slinging Sam's rifle over one shoulder, the mad veteran strode to the ditch edge above Sam and raised the old Indian War days cavalry saber, as Ival had seen it raised in ceremonies honoring his father and other war dead.

To shoot Sam and bring pursuers was what a disoriented killer might have done. To kill silently was the decision of a man who could, at least in this moment, think logically, and Ival hesitated, thinking of the man the mad soldier might have been before the war—the man he might, after treatment, again become.

An instant to shoot or to let the saber avenge childhood beatings and restore land to its rightful owners, Ival's dead parents' Indian bloodlines, Ival aimed and, bright blade already arcing, squeezed the trigger, bullet shattering the madman's spine, Sam's head already dropping, neck stump spurting blood.

Just too late or subconscious decision, Ival wasn't sure. Guilty or only pitying, he stayed on the farm and worked through harvest, the smells of sweat and ripe corn the smells of sanity. Then, he found a renter for his half of the farm, and for that of the widow and the child of a man who'd been kind sometimes, sometimes cruel, maybe crazed by his own war—the man Ival's mother had married, and given Ival the only brother he had ever known.

Following a Medicine Path begun before his Indian ancestors crossed from Asia to a world as new for them as it would be, generations later, for invading Europeans, Ival studied archaeology. His children's children's inheritance would not be land, but a knowledge of belonging in Creation, a knowledge as enduring as life-sustaining earth, as ephemeral as the fragrance of corn ripening after first frost.

# Silver Mercedes and Big Blue Buick: An Indian War

Tea McKenzie was driving her college-days' friend's big Buick through narrow Bavarian streets, and half asleep beside his insistently German-American but inescapably part-Sioux Indian wife, Mac McKenzie was memory-tripping through thirty years, to when he'd entered Germany the same way his English great-great-great-grandpappy had entered the New World, as a conqueror.

Though true to his menopausally moody mate—and true to the straight-arrow reputation a small-town businessman had to maintain—Mac was still, by God, a Man's Man—fifty-six years young—and he felt the pride of sexual conquests here, among his country's enemies. Despite Tea's fingernail's clicking like a huffy chicken's beak against the steering wheel, he could not stop staring at girls' nearly bare butts, rising from bicycle seats to put on more speed, to get around the car ahead—to put, Mac thought, a stronger shield than thin cloth between young curves and the curved fenders of the big car, which Tea was driving dangerously close.

Afraid that wine—which had made him happy and witty—might make his always unreasonably jealous wife misjudge distance, Mac drove after lunch, even though he hadn't agreed to borrowing this car and had sworn he would never risk driving in Europe, where he had done his share of damage, "with cannon, and with prick," as he'd told his best salesman, a handsome heartbreaker, clever with words and able to appreciate the manliness of joking about war and women—also quick to learn that sexually suggestive advertising and sexually insinuating sales talk sold shoes and just about everything else in America. His own love-life for too damned long consisting of joshing girls he hired because they were pretty enough to at least bend if not break customers' hearts, Mac had at first been cautiously favorable to taking this trip, hopeful that Tea was suggesting the romantic European second honeymoon she'd envied friends for taking, and he had trotted out photos that showed what he'd married, the taut butt, sweater-swelling boobs, and little girl smile that had made Miss Dorotea Weiss a Miss Iowa contestant, dark among New Ulm's blondes, but a worthy wife for one of the town's most up-and-coming young businessmen.

"Honeymoon, my eye!" Tea had said. "I want to get to know my husband, and I want to get to know our roots, yours and mine." With Indians nowhere near the top of the U.S. totem pole, Germany was the land that held the only roots Tea chose to acknowledge—Crazy Horse or Crazy Hitler her choices, Mac had thought. Disappointed one time too many, a little drunk and fed up to the teeth with trying to humor his wife, he'd told her in no uncertain terms, "You can get to know me better—and cheaper—at home, where my roots have been ever since my forefathers dug out your Indian roots, like weeds." His family album's neat rows bloomed with pale English petals, but there must have been one Irishman, with the gift of Blarney, to pass down the witty way with words. "My people were in the Mississippi skin trade," he'd told his wife, as he'd told a recent Chamber of Commerce crowd, "and as long as skins are used for shoes, I'll keep on in the skin trade, right here in New Ulm, Iowa, in the good old U. S. of A., where we belong." Hoping that would end it, he had offered to order more wine, but Tea had shaken her head, the hair she'd stopped dyeing the last few months hitting her empty glass with a dry sound like that of bugs against a lighted bulb. Fearing she'd have another breakdown, he'd agreed he'd apply for their passports, book airline tickets to London, and begin to do what he'd not planned to do until after he was old and feeble—train his best salesman, almost a son, to run the store.

A Dover pub woman with eyes as brown and sparkly as the beer she'd served had started to tell Mac about cannon shells crossing the Channel when she'd still been a schoolgirl, but Tea had interrupted, "My husband was an artilleryman," as if he'd been one of the Nazis.

"My forefathers came from England, maybe from somewhere right around here," he'd said. Then, having knocked back two pints, he'd defiantly stared south of where prim blouse lapels went north, and he had tipped generously.

On the boulevards of *Pair-ee*, he'd offered to buy Tea new duds and a new hairdo—and hair dye—to look like a beauty queen again and knock out some envious eyes back home. But, no, from the many shops whose windows displayed lingerie as vivid as bridal petals, Tea had bought a big straw hat. In it, her gray hair looked like the stems of a dead plant flared out from under an overturned basket. The hatband read "French Riviera," but tourist posters' topless-bathing-suited backs were all Mac was going to see of the Mediterranean.

"I'm sick of garlicky Frenchmen plunking themselves down beside me on trains without even asking, and most of them swarthier than the redskin cousins my redcoat husband won't let me forget," Tea had said, and had accepted—riding roughshod over Mac's objections—her Paris-based college friend's offer of a car.

On the road for a quick looksee at Dachau's concentration-camp exhibits, amid milk-cow-polka-dotted slopes as green as those along the Mississippi, Mac had tried to make the best of a not exactly joyous vacation by speaking a little *Deutsche*, and appreciative waitresses, as pretty as cheerleaders at home, had let his gaze do whatever it would when they'd bent for coins he'd left on trays.

Droplets of lake water glittering like showgirl sequins, he'd quipped—to an Englishman, he'd thought, but unsmiling Swede, it'd turned out—"Why Bikini? That was just a test. Why not the real thing? Why not Hiroshima bra and Nagasaki panties?"

That night, low-cut-blouse-wearing, tip-seeking waitresses bowing to serve him, he, like the damned fool optimist any store owner had to be to make a sale, had tried arousing Tea by sharing some sexy memories of what he'd lived between battles.

"So, you lied when you told me I was the first."

Prostitutes didn't really count, he'd tried to convince her—though some had been students, fiancées, even wives, before starvation began. Anyway, persuading Tea that he'd been as inexperienced as herself was no more false than sales pitches about ladies' shoes, and with money rolling in, she'd never asked how it was earned.

"Your redskin whore, that's all I've been all these years."

"Nosiree," he'd told her. "Like you've always said, you're as white as I am. You were a beauty queen, don't forget, and you'd still be a damned good-looking woman if you dressed up and got some hair-color renewer. I saw your friend's hubby staring at your boobs while showing you how to drive his car."

"'Daddy used to call me a German princess and tell me our fatherland was so clean you could eat off the cobblestones," she'd said. "But we're almost to where Walt Disney's swan castle is, and cows are pooing in the streets."

He knew that the cobblestones would soon be hosed clean, but seizing his chance, he'd asked why not spend some time in reportedly cleanly Switzerland and start having fun. "No," she'd said, she would push on into Germany as far as he had pushed, adding, "I lost World War Two, and I mean to see where I lost it."

"I wrote you V-mail letters whenever I could. I came home to you, only you. I think I surrendered to the wrong woman," he'd told her, drunk and fed up, after she'd whined it was what whores had done to her "boy" that kept the children from coming, never mind that it might have been her fault, not his. "My babies dead in my womb as sure as if they'd been atom-bomb radiated. All because you liked lording it over poor young German women, *my* people, and you had no religion to control your drunken lust."

"It was the only life I had while *your people* were doing their damndest to end my life altogether," he'd told her, having drunk too much to be able to keep his trap shut. "Wearing a rubber and then squeezing a tubeful of prophylactic up my dick wasn't fun, but it kept me from bringing you any disease."

A man had to stick up for himself, he'd told himself, but he knew he should never have mentioned his past, and he should never have argued.

"Her doting father; a jealous, timid mother; your refusing to adopt a child because, so she says, most up for adoption were Indian; and now, menopause—just humor her and hope for the best," the counselor had counseled, accepting his check as if it was perfectly OK to charge an arm and a leg for hope.

Only one more week to grit the teeth and be patient, and then, home—money to make, high school soon to start, girls hiking their skirts when trying on shoes, this goddamned, tiring trip just memories, *and stories*, of *fräuleins* with snowy breasts as big as alps.

He was relaxed by noontime wine and was sleepy enough to consider asking Tea to take the wheel, but with a lake ahead, they were stalled behind a line of tour buses, brief-skirted and even-briefer-bathing-suited young women bicycling between cars, and, Tea ominously silent beside him, he kept the wheel even after huge buses turned, like elephants following their leader, to the first beach. With only spindly foreign cars ahead, the Buick seemed, as army trucks had seemed, too wide for the narrow, twisting road.

Blindingly bright high beams flashing in the rearview mirror, a silver Mercedes sped around three cars and cut in to avoid an oncoming truck. Mac kicked the brake so hard his wound-stiffened ankle hurt, and grabbed Tea's arm, which was trying to kill them both, he feared—but she was only sending a fusillade of blasts from the Buick's loud horn.

Damned near jammed against the rear of a little Fiat, the Mercedes' driver pushed sunglasses up onto hair as silver as his car, flung a smug, blue-eyed glance back, and, jeweled ring flashing, gave Tea the finger.

"Older than I am, and hugging that young, bare-shouldered woman and driving like a teenage boy, the pig!" Tea snorted.

Pig my eye! Hot dog! Mac thought gleefully, feeling no call to be insulted since he hadn't honked the horn, feeling complicity in a man's right to hold his own, and feeling tickled pink at seeing that a man his age could get a young woman. Hot dog!

For miles, bright brake lights flashed again and again ahead, but when the next village slowed traffic, Mac saw the long, silver car pulling over to park, only a block ahead.

"As haughty as an American millionaire," Tea muttered, taking off the French Riviera hat to fan her face. "If Indians had been paid for losing their war, I'd be rich."

Mac kept silent. All these years, she'd only claimed her German people.

Traffic barely moving, Tea jumped out, slamming the door on his cry and awkwardly running—but, high heels not meant for speed, the Buick soon caught up with her. She had arrived too late, thank God. Mercedes left half on sidewalk, half in traffic, the silver-haired man and his bare-shouldered blond had disappeared behind one of the sun-silvered store windows.

When Mac honked, the American horn loud over little horns tooting behind him, Tea got into the car even before he could bring it to a complete stop, and as she buckled her seat-belt, he saw a gleam like puddled water in her pink-flowered lap—the Mercedes' front-door mirror.

The Mercedes man hadn't seen Tea monkeying with his car, Mac hoped. When he said, trying to sound mad as hell, "I'd like to punch that guy's nose," Tea remained silent, a sign of her menopausal worst. Then, a girl cycling past on the right side, wind lifting short green skirt, Mac heard his wife muttering, "Sixteen when I met you"—all he could hear, enough to make him resolve not to let her drive, no matter how tired he got.

This was what he'd feared, what other returning veterans had warned against—driving a big car in narrow streets, when most Germans drove tiny Volkswagens, or caught buses, or bicycled or walked.

Bright lights flashing, he saw the silver Mercedes swerving in and out of the long line of cars behind him, and he tried to remember how many kilometers made how many miles to the Austrian border. Too many, was all he could think. His shirt was soaked. His pants stuck to his legs. And there would be town after sweltering town. "That German is trying to catch up, and his damned mirror will land us behind bars," he said, calmly but in a firm voice. "Throw it out the window!"

"Like fun I will," Tea muttered. "If he drives alongside again, I'll hold this mirror right up and show that haughty old pig how he looks beside that young woman."

"Do what I tell you, you crazy bitch . . ." Like a damned fool, he'd let himself get tired, let himself get pushed too far, and he'd said it. The truth. "Crazy." That and "old" the two things the counselor had said he must never say. "I'm just trying to take care of my baby girl, not let her sauciness get her into trouble, more trouble than I can fix," he tried, more scared when he heard fear thinning his voice.

"Crazy," Tea said very quietly, her words almost lost in the shriek of tires as the Mercedes wedged between the two cars behind them. "Almost kill us, just to block traffic in the next town. Crazy."

"But there are laws. This is a democracy, now, like the U.S. They'll put you in jail."

"Crazy," she said. "Spend all that money blowing this country to bits, then spend more putting it back together. And that gray-haired pig treats us like we were the ones who surrendered."

"Hide the mirror under the seat. Please."

She waved it, catching the sun and causing the driver right behind them to honk.

"Crazy," she said. "I know who's crazy. A sex maniac. Girls young enough to be his daughters, if he was capable of having any, if he was man enough, if he ever spent any time at home with his wife and not just blowing the smell of beer in her face and snoring in bed." He strained sweat-blurred eyes to see past the huge truck just ahead, but there was only steep mountain wall, no side road, and as he rounded a curve, the Mercedes drew alongside. Sunglasses as round as double-barreled shotgun muzzles aimed forward, free arm still locked around the blond's bare shoulders, the silver-haired man sped past, passed the truck, and vanished over a hill. If the German had noticed his missing mirror, he hadn't connected it with Tea's angry tooting and this big blue car. She had been lucky yet again. And she took her luck—the same damned way she took her hardworking, generous husband—for granted.

"I want us to get out of town, get out of the old ruts and get to know one another," Tea had said, imitating psychology lingo in demanding this trip; but Mac thought that he knew Miss Dorotea Weiss already—too well. It wasn't just menopause, in his opinion. Like most pretty women, Tea had always gotten her way—with her father, with teachers, and with her boyfriends. Raised on a piddly little farm, rented from a family who'd owned several ever since they'd clobbered Tea's half-breed mother's Indian people, Tea had never had good clothes to show off her good looks, but a movie-starlet face and a sexy body had gotten her everything, including, by golly, Mac McKenzie.

With milk cows and pigs and garden stuff on the farm, Tea hadn't been hungry during the Depression, and she couldn't appreciate that her husband had had to work hard and butter up the town bigwigs who could help him rise. Thanks to family money and college, those men had been officers in the war. Now, like their fathers before them, they ran New Ulm, the U.S., and the world. Look at Germany, look at the silver-haired man's young blond. The war no more than a fraternity-party scuffle, everything was hunky-dory again.

Mac had sucked up to bosses and had risen to own his own store. Not bad for a man whose father had worked in a factory. And Tea's dieting and dressing to look great had helped his career.

Calling her crazy had certainly not been smart, he had to admit, but at least he hadn't called her old, to let her know that she was not the beauty queen she'd been, a fact that expensive counseling and all the makeup she used to use hadn't changed, and sure as hell, her not dyeing her hair lately hadn't helped. Another lake shimmering ahead, a young woman bicycling around the Buick, he forced himself to turn his eyes from bare back and scarcely clothed rear, but Tea was already staring at him as she'd stared at the Mercedes man. "I could only afford two years of college," she sobbed. "I wasted my life, helping you get what people expected you to get, a new car every year and all the rest. I'm worse off than my poor mother—away from her people, working like a horse—but at least she died thinking she'd made my life better."

"You're darn tooting your life is better," Mac told her. "Your dad never took your mother beyond New Ulm, let alone on a trip like this."

"Like this," Tea said, in the new, calm voice, and leaning against him, lovingly it momentarily seemed, she stamped her high-heeled left foot down, astraddle his right foot, on the accelerator.

Bicycle and bare body thrown up between car and truck, Mac's left foot lifted over the clutch pedal and slammed the brake.

Bikini-clad butt dented blue steel a hands-width from the windshield, and pale waist flesh quivered above a black waistband.

Someone helped the girl to slide over a fender, and she ran to look at her twisted bike. Tea had been lucky again, Mac thought—her luck his quick thinking and his quick left foot.

"I'm not young anymore," she sobbed against his chest. "My looks were all you cared about, and nine months, six, five, then you'll be free of your old worn-out squaw, free to have all the sex you want, and it won't matter one iota. To you I'm already as dead as my babies are."

"I'll pay for a new bike and a little something extra for good German-American relations," he said. Then, through his numbness, panic, and the habits of many years, he remembered "nine months—dead." "The best care there is, no matter if it costs me an arm and a leg. I'll do all I can for my baby girl," he told his wife, a sob in his voice as he remembered how pretty she had been; but, though artful with customers, he'd stayed honest with himself, and, always ready to find silver dollars lining the darkest clouds, he had to admit he'd feel relieved not to have to go on pampering Tea through old age, his hard-earned home her personal Indian reservation.

On the plus side, she'd been a loyal helpmeet, and she was still thinking of what would be best for him—"all the sex you want." Other widowers, still Men's Men in vigorous middle age, had remarried and kept community respect. Maybe he'd find a wife—a good-looker, but not another vain beauty queen, and not another not-quite-vanished Vanishing American—all that bottled-up hate about stuff so long ago nobody could remember. Maybe he'd start a family. He hadn't seen a doctor, and nothing had been proved. Maybe he'd live long enough to raise a son, who'd learn the business from his old dad. Tea might be as jealous as hell, up there in her German-Lutheran heaven, but maybe she'd also feel good, knowing that she'd given her husband a child after all, in a way—a 100 percent white American boy.

Reckoning, short range, what a bicycle cost—long range, Tea's life insurance—Mac felt able to put on his Sale Days smile and do whatever he had to do; but as he stepped from the car, sweaty shoulder blades flattened against hot steel to let traffic pass, he felt the passenger door jolt open.

Before he could sidle around the front bumper, shoes crunching headlight glass, Tea had grabbed the girl she'd already damned near killed.

"Don't, you crazy bitch! They'll put us in jail and throw away the key!" Mac yelled, everyone looking at him as if he was the crazy one, as if he'd been to blame. The girl put her head on Tea's shoulder, and Tea, her dark face all but buried in blond hair, began to sob.

Picking up Tea's Riviera-banded hat and placing it between the propped-up bicycle's handlebars, someone put money into the hat and added silver to weight the paper down. Other people patting the girl's bare shoulders and contributing, there was quite a wad by the time Mac emptied his wallet, mumbling, "Sorry, Sorry," telling his wife, telling men, women, and children he'd killed, telling the young soldier he had been—"Sorry, Sorry"—nothing going to change, nothing he could do, nothing—crying, crying like a goddamned fool.

# The New World Invades the Old

Army translator Sher Sheridan witnessed the torture of an elderly Filipino tribesman and, sickened by the sight of knives moving over skin as brown as that of his father, wished it was U.S. imperialism's contemporary commander staked to the earth floor of the interrogation tent. Sher's angry wish was rooted in ordinary human sympathy, and in knowledge that white invaders had taken his Nez Perce people's homeland, raped women, and mingled their blood with his family's blood. Also, he'd lost his white fiancée to a white college classmate, whose politician father had kept him out of the war.

The elderly Filipino, his native language probably his only means for screaming that he was not a Japanese spy, might still have saved his life if he'd hidden what he felt about those whose bombs had destroyed his village.

Sher had learned to hide his feelings—from white schoolyard bullies, from teachers angered by an Indian janitor's kid's being more intelligent than themselves, and from racist soldiers fighting for the army of democracy.

In a college research paper, Sher had compared Chief Joseph's heroic retreat with that of Moses. No parting of any Red Sea for the Nez Perce men, women, and children—mountain snow had been God's only intercession, and the hard-won deliverance had been lost when bluecoats swarmed from warm railway coaches to block the exodus short of Canada. Sher's research had impressed a professor, but knowledge of a skillful retreat—led not by a war chief but by a peace chief, a diplomat—was knowledge that would, Sher knew, not make army officers accept any Indian as an equal. To the camouflage blotching of combat-fatigues and helmets, soldiers added real jungle foliage, and to the name with which his parents had sought to hide Indian blood, Sheridan, Sher, adroit with words, added an obedient, good-soldier way of speaking and acting.

After Japan's surrender, Japanese language ability was required for the army of occupation, and Sher, fluent in college-and-army-inculcated Japanese, stayed on in Japan as a civil-service employee, translating for generals and for American businessmen looking to translate victory into profits.

His impassioned V-mail-compressed American English had not persuaded his fiancée to wait for him, but "Money talks" was an American slogan, and American money convinced prostitutes to endure sex more like rape than love.

Sher planned to go on earning his living as a translator, but then his parents were killed in a car crash, and after the funeral, he extended his leave of absence and returned to university study, including smatterings of Greek, Italian, Spanish, German, and Russian. The army's slogan "If you can't lick 'em, join 'em" still his hope for physical, if not spiritual, survival, he took his degree in French, "the language of diplomacy," and, finding the one employer then legally required to hire an Indian as an equal, began a State Department career.

Every day, he translated the terms with which inept political appointees and their capable underlings maintained the economic dominance won by war. During many nights, weekends, and occasional vacations, he made love to diplomats' daughters or wives who found his dark face "exotically handsome" and his manners "charmingly French."

The bed was his battleground, but he'd learned that the only wars won were ones not fought, and his victories were platonic loves, which resurrected the youth he'd been before his first love had betrayed him while he'd been enduring the dangers and the horrors of war. Whether platonic or erotic, his conquests always ended with his, or with his lover's, being moved to another diplomatic post.

"My wife-to-be was young. I was young. And we were separated by my duty to my country," was his diplomatically acceptable answer, in whichever of his languages, to the question often put—put by the women most like him, women seeking vengeance against unfaithful husbands or lovers. Sher thought that his orgasms, described by a socialite wife from Kansas as "tornadic," were actually attacks by warrior hordes of massacred ancestors' never-to-be-born descendants, the lingering afterglow the lulls between Indian uprisings.

"Yes, some day," was a diplomatic reply to "But don't you want to marry and have children?" The interrogators were women for whom neither marriage nor children meant more than maintaining a politically acceptable status.

Her seduction utterances the excoriation of her lobbyist husband, a woman near forty murmured, in postcoital contentment, her delicately beautiful face's purple-lipsticked lips barely parting, "You must be thirty-some, and you mustn't wait too long, or your 'someday' for wife and children will never appear on any calendar." Her words kindled a new urgency in him, an urgency that provoked an all-night Indian rampage, the historic consequence of which amounted to an American diplomat's translator's translating, unshaven and unbathed, and mispronouncing so many words he caused a usually poker-faced Russian diplomat to smile triumphantly.

Now considered a stereotypical drunken—and inconveniently hung over—Indian, and therefore a possible weak spot in America's diplomatic front, Sher was offered his choice among three postings less vital to American interests than the United Nations at Lake Success.

Picturing tourist-poster women whose complexions were like those of Indians, Sher chose "the cradle of democracy," Greece—which had converted its woodlands into ships and built an economy based on piracy—as America was now converting minerals into nuclear missiles.

In an Athens hotel room with a Russian woman, whose sexual wiles could not quite conceal a geopolitical intent, Sher's emotional balance was as precarious as that of his ouzo glass, nervously placed before him by slender fingers—one's skin untanned where a wedding band had recently been. Declaring that Czarist Russia had oppressed her own people, from a Siberian population, the woman professed hatred for what America had done to Indians.

"All too long ago to matter," Sher lied loudly for the microphone concealed in his CIA-supplied wristwatch, and for the KGB tape recorder no doubt receiving transmissions from an oversized, unproletarian necklace. Fighting his own battle, Sher, the self-conceived sex guerilla, murmured diplomatically, "Because you and I are intelligent and use words well, we have the privilege of serving our respective nations; but we have so much in common, we know that the U.S.-Soviet Cold War's like the collision of two glaciers, which will disappear into mingling tropical tides."

She responded, "Yes. We respect and take for granted one another's loyalties, but with us the antagonisms of the world struggle are naturally forgotten."

Contriving to switch drinks while rescuing his glass from a table edge vibrated by an electric fan, Sher offered a toast to the peaceful harmony he and his sister translator were helping to make possible for his nation and hers. Respecting the truth of what he'd just artfully uttered—respecting the innocent boy he'd once been—and expressing the platonic love he felt for a woman whose situation was so much like his own, he put a pillow over her necklace while she was sipping drugged ouzo and babbling information into his wristwatch. She knew little. Like himself, she was not supposed to have information; her duty was to obtain information. She had failed, and he could only hope that her failure might not harm her and harm the husband and children of whom she'd spoken lovingly.

Once she had fallen asleep, he placed his pillow beside hers, dented the shape of his head into it, and the time-telling part of his wristwatch telling him that it was midnight in the land where democracy had supposedly first dawned, he told his unconscious bedmate's necklace's largest fake pearl, "I respect the fact that we have spent an entire night together with nothing said by either of us that could interest our nations' spies"; wrote a note professing gratitude for a night of friendship, without sex; and caught a taxi to another hotel, not guessing that the move would end his war with women.

A brochure had called Sher's escape haven "totally Greek," which proved to be half accurate. The hotel had dubbed its small bar The London Pub, but the fifty-some-year-old proprietor and his hauntingly sad thirty-or-less-year-old wife were Greek.

Encountered in the hallway, after her husband had driven off to resupply the bar with English beer, the wife pleaded, "Won't you take me to bed?"

His surprised "Of course" encouraged her to add, "Without contraceptives. I have to have a son."

His abrupt reversal, from acceptance to refusal, loosed an explanation of a marriage not blessed by pregnancy. The only solution for a Greek man with a name and a business to pass on would be to divorce and take a new wife, despite doctors' saying that he was the one who was infertile.

The same pride that rejected medical opinion would inflict crude surgery on a cuckolding American Indian, Sher thought, and he diplomatically lied that he was married, adding, "Happily."

"And I also am happily married," his suppliant pleaded. "But to save my marriage I must have a son, and you are dark like a Greek, dark like my husband."

Dropping her broom, she pulled first apron and then dress off over her head, and her hair a tumultuous, glistening black like that of Sher's first love, a confusion of passion, compassion, and loneliness inspired an afternoon of sex, which only ended with the sound of the Greek hotel owner's Italian delivery vehicle's bringing a case of English ale.

Sher spent his weekends in the hotel until he learned that his first child would be a loving Greek couple's son—a son whom Sher, stationed in Israel, then Egypt, then France, could occasionally visit, even after he was married, with a son and daughter at home in the Wallowa Mountains of Oregon, U.S.A., his Indian War against the women of invading Caucasians won by becoming the diplomatic and the human ideal, a peaceful solution.

# Two Wars, Two Loves, Two Shores, and an Ocean on Fire

Headlights false dawns in trees, between Ayun's bedroom window and a nightclub up the street, birds started trilling, confusing the manmade and the natural—as did most Caucasian Americans, Ayun thought—the thought itself instilled by university study, not spontaneous, not natural. He thought of his father's farming the Indian way, plowing nutrients back into the land, while neighboring whites burned off corn stalks and oat stubble to make plowing easier. He thought of animals' mating only in the season that enabled newborns to survive, and he thought of humans' mating year-round and mingling sex with their dream of a hereafter.

When automobile engines ceased, Ayun heard a singer tremulously lamenting her unfaithful sailor sweetheart, her language the one that Columbus had brought to the New World, the language that Ayun had first heard, murmured in his ear, during World War Two, when he'd been a seventeen-year-old merchant-marine seaman.

Dance after dance, his girl's perfumed hair tangled with the mustache he'd started so that he would look less like an Indian and more like a suave movie star. Then, "The Star Spangled Banner" ending the night's dancing, he escorted his partner home, through streets that, she'd hinted, might be dangerous.

"Hey, Sailor, you got a girl, I got whiskey," a soldier offered from a parked car.

"She's my wife," Ayun said, and, a poignantly small hand clasping his until the drunken soldier drove off, he felt a truth beyond the lie he'd told, felt a future he might not ever live.

At the next corner, glimpsing two dark figures following, he gripped rolls of quarters to weight his fists. Both men crossed the street and disappeared.

"I guess they saw that I know how to fight," he laughed, feeling cocky, though the quarter trick was one a shipmate had taught him and one he had never used.

"They were checking to see that you're not lighter-skinned than I am," his girl told him. "They beat up gringos who mess around with neighborhood girls."

A few blocks further, a skinny body lay on a lawn, pale face and silver-wings insignia dimly reflecting a distant streetlight. Shaking the airman didn't wake him. He didn't smell of alcohol; but, if he was drunk, calling police might send him to jail.

Ayun intended to check again after he'd seen his girl safely home; but, learning that he'd have to catch three different buses to get back to his ship, her parents invited him to stay and sleep in the room that had belonged to their two sons, both gone to war.

The airman would sober up and be OK, Ayun decided, and the man he'd left to live or die became as unreal as a battle-casualty statistic.

Her parents gone to bed, Ayun's new girlfriend offered a midnight snack—peanut butter and homemade jam on homemade bread, with one of her father's beers. Nervous from having had to be polite with the parents, a beer was just what Ayun needed, but since his girl poured milk for herself, he left the beer capped and said he'd have what she was having.

A thin white outline already rimming violet lipstick, his first taste of sweet milk was his girl's kissing him, her dark eyes shut tight, her mouth not quite finding his, her delicate upper lip between his lips.

He bowed for a full kiss just as her tongue began moving, murmuring, "Thanks for having milk with me, instead of beer."

Ayun and his girl kissed more and more passionately, until she whispered, "Mustn't quit talking too long, or Daddy will worry."

The table creaking when she started to cut bread, she mumbled, dark eyes down, "The crust is a little hard. Would you finish cutting?"

He kissed her sweat-salty palm's welts, gouged by the knife haft, then pressed the blade into the cut she'd started in the bread and began to saw, back and forth, back and forth, the table creaking. Worried that noise would wake the parents, he hurriedly cut the first piece of bread and started the second, cutting faster and faster, creaking of table louder and louder.

A door banged open; but instead of coming into the kitchen, the father's heavy footfalls and the mother's hesitant steps went straight to the bedroom that was waiting for Ayun.

Dark eyes fixed on her hands, Ayun's girl continued spreading red jam, tinting peanut butter the color of her blushing skin.

After a long time of whispering, only the mother came into the kitchen and, her blush as deep as that of her daughter, said, "Don't stay up late, talking. Tomorrow is early mass."

When Ayun got into bed, he was embarrassed about what the parents had thought, and felt guilty because he'd wanted their thought to be true. He was tired, but the squeaking of the bed every time he rolled over startled him awake.

"'AIRMAN STRUCK WITH CLUB DIES,'" the girl's father read in his morning paper. "Only a few blocks from here, but he might as well have been in combat over Germany."

Ayun said nothing, but he thought that the airman might have lived if he'd gotten help.

"Thank you, Ayun, for seeing our daughter safely home," the mother said, and probably assuming from his skin that he was Hispanic and Catholic, she invited him to attend early mass.

He lied that he had Sunday shipboard work. Then, the girl he so desperately loved beautiful in white shoes, white gloves, and white dress, he met dark, long-lashed eyes' loving gaze, and despite military secrecy, told the truth—that he would, within hours, sail off to war.

For days, that war was salt spray in coffee and tear-blurred eyes strained, in wind, to scrutinize endlessly cresting and subsiding waves. He sounded alerts again and again, only to be told that the periscopes he'd spotted were really stub branches of trees, which storms had torn out of New England's thin earth and launched into the ocean. Depth charges, hurled from American destroyers and British corvettes, exploded in the distance and destroyed, or failed to destroy, submarines.

Ayun carried wooden boxes of machine-gun ammunition to the anti-aircraft guns, and carried cannon shells, which were at first so slippery with frost, he'd almost drop them, and then so firmly frozen to his thick mittens that gunners had to pry and twist to get them loose before they could load their guns. After battle drills were completed, he carried his loads back to where they were stored, protected from corrosive saltwater. The heavy work was like carrying bales of hay to cattle on his parents' farm, except for having to time his steps so as not to slip off the icy and constantly rising and falling deck's steep slants and into a sea so cold the only rescue instruction was, "Grab the heaviest thing you can find and drown with the least amount of suffering."

After their part of the convoy left the protection of patrolling warships, planes attacked them, off the coast of German-occupied Norway, and Ayun's first sea fight was a repetition of the battle drills; but after a lengthy engagement, which concluded with no ships sunk and no planes shot down, there was less ammunition to carry back into storage.

Bombs and machine parts unloaded onto Red Army trucks, the interpreter, a black-haired, blue-eyed woman of maybe thirty, noticed Ayun's dark skin and high cheekbones. "I speak Russian, but I'm Sami," she told him. "We are reindeer herders, overwhelmed by Europeans centuries ago, just as your Indian people were. Now, ours is a nation within other nations. I work for the Russians, but I haven't forgotten that they burned our ceremonial drums and burned our priests. So did the Norwegians, the Swedes, and the Finns, but we Sami survived, and we will outlast the Nazis, too."

Burning, freezing, or drowning likely to be his future, shy goodbye kisses from a girl in Galveston his only love life since high school's smooching and petting, Ayun kissed the Sami woman, and after guiding him through his first sex, she guided him back to his ship in the strange, smoke-gray light of the Land of White Nights.

He had served for three years as a merchant seaman in World War Two, surviving submarine and bomber attacks and collisions with floating ice. Then, since he'd not been in one of the regular branches of the armed forces, he was drafted, and was captured after his third fire fight in Korea. Hearing Russian being spoken outside a tent, whose only warmth came from his and other prisoners' bodies, he'd remembered the Sami woman, unbuttoned but not undressed, in a cold room, dimly lit by a sun that was actually months from dawning. I am Cherokee, he had silently echoed the Sami woman's words. If the Great Spirit wills it so, I will survive, and my future children will survive.

Now, hearing birds trilling welcome after welcome, farewell after farewell, to the nightclub parking lot's sunups and sundowns, and hearing the Chicana nightclub singer tremulously lamenting lost love, he remembered perfumed hair's tangling with the mustache he'd grown so he'd look less like an Indian—remembered yearning to be someone his girl might marry, yearning to be a part of a people not doomed to become Vanishing Americans.

He had survived two wars, and two brief loves had helped him to mentally survive memories of friends bayoneted by prison guards, and memories of friends jumping from their blazing ship, oil spreading, ocean on fire, fins flaming like lamp wicks, the flames snuffed, as sharks seized struggling bodies and, like the submarines glistening among ice floes in the distance, dived.

# Raven Mocker Witches
# and Refugees

His first day as a university teaching assistant completed, payment of debts incurred during six years of study just begun, Ayun was about to enter the house he'd rented cheap, in Fresno, California's, Chicano ghetto, when two uniformed men strode up on either side.

"Let's see some photo I.D.," the bigger of the two ordered. Then, after Ayun showed his university identification card, he asked, politely, "You see anyone hiding in your alley, Professor? Or hear anyone speaking Mexican?"

Ayun heard and spoke Spanish every day in nearby markets, but remembering polite North Korean interrogators and others waiting with clubs, he politely lied, "I've heard and seen nothing."

Later, while watering his landlord's all-but-wilted rose bush, and admiring the beauty of a woman nursing her baby on the porch of a dead-vine-covered house across the street, he saw the two immigration cops drive past. Jammed into the police van's steel-barred rear section, a dozen men and women were being hauled back to a life of poverty in Mexico.

At dusk, whistling came from the bush-lined alley behind Ayun's backyard, and, a woman's tremolo whistle answering, a shadowy form slipped past Ayun's garage, then hurried across the street and into the dead-vine-covered house. Lonely, Ayun heard again and again whistling from the alley, and heard a fulfillment he yearned for—a woman's answering whistle.

He wondered if his Indian complexion and his college-course Spanish might let him pass for a Chicano in the neighborhood nightspot, whose bright lights and music were so enticingly close to where he spent sleepless hours alone; but he knew that he might get into a fight, be sent to jail, and maybe lose the job he'd studied six years to get.

Driving home at the end of his first month of work, he met four young Hispanic men striding down the middle of the street, their carefully combed, greased hair gleaming like black helmets. To avoid confrontation, he drove with two wheels up on the sidewalk to pass, and face set, not to show fear, he did what he'd done in high school, in the merchant marine, and in the infantry—he avoided meeting eyes.

Leaving a drooling green hose looped around a pink plastic lawn flamingo's neck, a pink-faced, pink-dressed, gray-haired neighbor fled into her pink house, and leaving her swing swaying on the porch of the dead-vine-covered house, the young mother, her shorts and nursing-bra flashes of white among shadows, disappeared as her door slammed shut.

Ayun parked his car in the driveway and walked slowly to his back door, but once he was inside and out of sight, he locked the door and hurried to the front drapes, which, following the orders of his landlord, he always kept drawn so no one would see what there was to steal. Opening a small slit of bright sunlight, he watched as, across the midday shimmer of the street, two of the young Hispanic men went around on either side of the dead-vine-covered house, while two others strode up to the front door.

Though both front and back doorbells of the dead-vine-covered house were ringing like burglar alarms, no one answered, and after shouting something through curtained windows, the four men swaggered off.

Teaching occupied Ayun's mind during the day, and after a while he forgot about the bellicose men, but at dusk, he'd hear a whistle from the alley behind his house and hear a woman's answering whistle.

From dreaming of rowing a lifeboat riddled by shrapnel, desperate to reach a distant ledge of ice, Ayun awoke, the sound in his ears not the Raven Mocker witch scream of a German dive-bomber, but the sound of a siren.

Parting his dimly lit living room's glowing drapes, he saw that the garage behind the dead-vine-covered house across the street was on fire. Flames threw the neighboring house's plastic flamingos' shadows across a glowing lawn, while real birds, startled from trees, circled, their wings' shadows those of the dive-bombers or the Raven Mocker witches he'd dreamed.

No lights came on in the dead-vine-covered house, despite a policeman's again and again ringing the bell. Firemen pushed a car out of the driveway and into the street, to get its gas tank further from the flames. They sprayed water onto sparks blown into the house's dead vines, but they let fire consume the garage before turning their hose on hissing embers.

After both emergency vehicles left, red and blue lights flashing, Ayun saw people rush from the dead-vine-covered house, the young nursing mother among them, her white-shorts-and-white-bra-banded body poignantly graceful and vulnerable against an open door's bright light. Her baby in her arms, she stared into the darkness for whoever might attack, while men and women hastily loaded rattling kitchen pans and loose piles of bedding and clothing into their car's trunk, frantic children clutching at parents' rapidly moving legs.

Finally, the house door open, light still on inside, the old car slowly moved off into darkness, its engine strained by so much weight.

For a long time, Ayun lay sleepless, thinking of the people fleeing whoever had torched the garage.

During World War Two's vast chaos, he had walked a beautiful Hispanic girl home, to a family in which he'd felt he'd belonged, for one night. Then, he'd loaded a ship with bombs, which would obliterate thousands of families. He thought of leaders making alliances and breaking alliances and killing thousands on thousands, terrified children clutching at the legs of terrified parents, who were packing what they could and fleeing, black shadows of wings circling flames, bombers or Raven Mocker witches plunging to tear out hearts, take years of lives.

# Campfire and Cone
of a Pine

Brown body mostly bare, blue bra and shorts shifting as she climbs into the jeep and onto her boyfriend's lap, the girl looks Indian, and that sure as hell isn't going to get her any respect, Hawk thinks.

I bet she'll do it tonight, Tom thinks, and he envies the boyfriend what he must be feeling, through thin cloth wet with sweat. Mountain wind blowing two black braids twisted like licorice Momma used to buy, Tom is almost able to taste how it would be if one flew into his mouth.

Highballing downhill, the deer Hawk shot bouncing on the hood of the Jeep, Claude is trying to think how to do what he has sure as hell got to do, but not be sent back to prison. The sissy-talking boyfriend is probably more queer than not, and would he, after more gin?—the Indian girl near naked, just asking for it—would the boy, in fuddled good feeling, share her with three new friends?—or, passed out, not know what they'd do to her—after getting her drunk—or, what the hell would she have to say about it once they had her spread and her man as unconscious from booze as from anybody's fists.

Would wishy-washy, fat Tom get excited and join the fun? Would Hawk—a redskin like the girl, and so quiet you never knew what the hell he was thinking?

Sexy, yes, god yes, she is sexy, with her pretty pair bouncing and jiggling in the rearview mirror every time the jeep hits a bump—sexy, and Claude is driving sober—sober enough—to let the others get drunk enough, and Claude is driving to find a campsite among trees so dense no forest-fire observer's binoculars could accidentally witness the romping and stomping between slender thighs.

Claude twists his rearview mirror into aim at the untanned curves tantalizingly emerging beyond the borders of shorts as the jeep jolts. Yes, oh, lord god yes, he's got to, he's just got to, with or without his buddies' help. And, sure, once he's had her they won't hold back. The girl will cry. And secretly love it, they always do. And if her boyfriend is passed out or pretending he is, she will not even tell him. She's not that dumb. None of them are.

She's worried about the three men, especially the big one, with a scar glistening red in bright sun between black whisker stubble and sunburned ear. She wishes her boyfriend hadn't accepted the ride, although she's higher up this mountain than they'd have gotten by hiking, the lake where they'd planned to spend the night a mile or more below, brilliant blue, as sky must have been in ancestors' time.

"I love you, but marriage, no," her boyfriend had said last night.

"Because I'm Indian?" she'd demanded; but no, he'd said, his teeth cutting gradually lengthening intervals of darkness between words. Natural to suspect racial considerations, but no, and it was not—not—because he'd had her virginity and had had her a year and didn't respect her. Sure, why shouldn't she enjoy her body—and enjoy his, or somebody else's —why not? And sure they'd been good together—those marathon spiritual raps at parties, or beautiful make-out dancing with others and home to his pad with the rhythm of an imaginary fertility-dance orgy still intense in the ease of marijuana and beer. And that they'd made it with other people when angry and offing each other wasn't the trouble either. There was no trouble, it was nothing new, it was just like he'd told her all along. He was simply not ready to marry—was still developing himself and wanted enough affairs to fully form his sexuality before he'd settle down with one woman and maybe, after a few years, marry, if it worked out.

"Why not with me?"

With me—in the family church, and Poppa and Momma hugging their educated pale-face son-in-law and their college-graduate only child.

"It just doesn't figure."

"Just doesn't what?"

"The time and travel I want to have—and college—psychology or maybe philosophy—six years at least; it figures you'll have a more-or-less permanent relationship by then. You should. You're twenty-two, and guys generally are looking for someone under twenty-six."

Oh, Christ, she'd thought, he's stupid. A year—and I've just heard his voice and not the voice in my own head.

"The fact that I love you is beautiful in itself. I'll always feel it was a high spiritual thing that our relationship attained to this level—and will ennoble us the rest of our lives, though we live with others."

"I don't love you."

"Well, plenty of times you've said you did. And now that I, too—"

"I was wrong."

"Well, I'm not wrong. I know my own mind. I love you. I stick by that. And I'll always carry the spiritual essence of our time together deep in my soul. It's interesting. Just when I knew for the first time that I'd experienced love—real love—for you, I immediately felt a high obligation to tell you that ours could never be a permanent relationship."

She tossed a pine cone into the fire and watched flames go low around it, then start to climb among dark seeds.

"All right, another of your moody periods. I'd finished talking anyway—except I was going to add that I want you again—this soon—because you told me you no longer love me."

"I never loved you."

"Maybe. Anyhow, I felt a surge of passion, a liberation, when hearing you say that you do not love me. It's a new complication in our relationship, that I love you and you don't love me. Getting it on together now would be beautiful—a lofty generosity on your part . . . magnanimity, a better word."

"Right. Your parents are both in advertising, but I'm a welder and a file clerk's daughter, and I've got simpler words."

"Don't apologize for your family. What words?"

"From now on, this is just a camping trip."

"She's spreading her sleeping bag the other side of the campfire from his," Claude said. "That makes it all the more sure."

"Great," Tom said. "She's high-grade quiff, Indian or not, like you say, Claude, and probably wants it—half naked like that and the boy drunk—sucking on our bottle like it was Momma's tit."

"Even if he wasn't drunk, he wouldn't say nothing but 'Yes, ma-an, yes,'" Claude said. "What else would he even be able to say—three of us and all with guns."

"Oh, but we ain't gonna—force her," Tom said. "I mean, we ain't like that. None of that rape stuff. I mean she'll cave in like ice cream, or we'll know if she really wants it *really*, whatever she says. Indian women they ain't no different than any other women—am I right, Hawk?"

"Count me out. I'm on parole," Hawk told dimwitted Tom as a way of telling Claude.

"The kid is smoking the old Mary Jane," Claude said, campfire blazing in pale eyes. "And he guzzled our booze plenty. He's a heavy-head, that kid, I can tell, I know the signs, and the girl, too, and, ma-an, on marijuana how they can wiggle their asses."

"Ma-an!" Tom mumbled and sneaked a second pull on the bottle before passing it back to his buddy Claude.

"So, hell, what would the Law say?" Claude said. "Us with steady jobs and paying taxes—these hippies, their word ain't nothing compared to ours. Yours too, Hawk, even if you are Indian. You been to jail, but like you say, it was just for fighting." "Count me out," Hawk told Claude and left it at that.

It's not my problem, he told himself, but when he heard her scream, as village girls had screamed in Korea—as his sister had screamed, their parents working night jobs, drunks raiding the reservation—he picked up his rifle.

"I should kill you," he'd told his wife.

"You should. I'd deserve it. But I was so lonesome with you off in the war. I'm sorry."

She'd stuck him for more monthly child support than he could earn, for a child that wasn't his—all because he'd believed "sorry" meant "sorry" and hadn't filed a countersuit.

Nearing the river, he couldn't hear screams, only water's roar, but shadows were struggling in the distant campfire's glow—the girl trying to fight loose from Claude, her boyfriend already tied to a tree.

Tom staggering behind her and hugging her around the legs to stop her kicking, Claude pulled off her sweatshirt and threw her onto the ground. Clawing, biting, she fought even after Claude slapped her twice—fought until he drove his fist into her solar plexus and she vomited.

Hawk hoped that the vomit would turn them off, but Claude only wiped her mouth with her sweatshirt and dragged her over to her sleeping bag.

Scared and sobered, Tom was out of it now and backing toward his rifle. Claude watched, one hand on his own rifle, the other hand clamped on long hair, while Tom took his gun and ran back toward their own camp.

One shot, even from this distance, might have scared them enough at the start, but now Claude was keeping his rifle close and was alert, half his mind on the girl, half his mind on Tom's maybe coming back, maybe with Hawk.

The girl was spunky, still fighting, weak as she was.

Her teeth flashed, biting Claude's wrist, and Claude knocked her out, deciding to have her limp if no other way.

She'd fought as if she had something to lose.

Claude was unlacing her boots in order to take off the blue jeans she'd put on when the night had turned cold.

Hawk saw teeth gleam and knew the boy had seen him get to his feet and was shouting, "Hurry," which was, of course, just great—Claude looking up at the kid to ask him who the hell he thought he was shouting at, but Claude's voice, too, was lost in the water's roar.

The sound of stumbling footfalls over rocks would be lost in that roar, too, Hawk thought. But Claude was getting up to have a look around, rifle in hand. Keeping in his mind the distance to a tree overhanging the river, Hawk slipped down the bank into chill current, feet first, floating on his back, rifle held high.

The first twigs glowing, reflecting campfire glow above him, he clamped one hand around his rifle, and with the other hand reached. A branch jerked through his fingers and damned near pulled his shoulder out of its socket but slowed him; he grabbed another. It broke. But the third grab spun him around and into rock-bottomed shallows.

His mind on the girl, spread motionless beneath his big body, Claude heard water squishing in a boot and looked up, scared, just as rifle butt struck skull.

Jet bombers screamed low over the mountain, their tailpipes leaving short meteor-trails, their navigation lights bright planets, and after the thunder of the bombers had ceased, a coyote howled its thanks to stars that were staying where they belonged.

The girl asked Hawk why he had left her boyfriend to walk out with Tom and Claude.

"Do you want him along?"

"No."

"Neither do I."

"I don't want you," she told him. "That's not what I meant when I said I didn't want him along."

"It's not what I meant either." He thought of his sister's being dragged into the back seat of somebody's car, thought of Korean women surrounded by troops while he'd stayed at a distance, feeling gutless and feeling humiliated—thought of his wife's lawyer's psyching him out as too damned weak to stand up for himself.

"I don't like being with sons of bitches," he said, just that. Later, sitting beside a fire and cooking deer liver spitted on a stick, he explained that he would need the day or two the others would be walking back— had to quit his job, get his pay, leave Claude's jeep for him—then hit the road. Claude would be out for revenge. "From me, too, I suppose."

"Maybe." He figured her boyfriend would give her name and address fast enough if threatened.

"It's strange. I'm the victim and you helped me, but we are the ones who have to become fugitives."

"You could call the cops," he told her, "but I suppose you got to think of your folks and friends." A college girl like her—he supposed she'd forgot what it was to be Indian. He supposed it was her nice gentle folks and nice safe home in her head that made her feel it was strange to have to cut out, where Christ, if she'd been raised on his reservation or if she'd been just behind the lines in Korea, she'd know this was everyday stuff.

"Hawk, would it keep you from having to leave your job and skip town if I went to the police?"

"Maybe." Claude's lawyer would put the girl through shit. Did she expect the jury—those ladies and gentlemen of the jury—to believe a girl like her had had to be forced? No mention that she was Indian, only the suggestion. Hadn't she maybe been drinking a bit? A bit, yes. Maybe more than a bit? No. No? Oh, well—but drinking—a bit, anyway, out there in that lonely place with those four men—four men.

"I'd have to skip town anyway, no matter what you decide," Hawk told the girl. "But don't you have to be here for college?"

"I tried four semesters, and my grades weren't great. Anyway, I need to leave. That boy and a few other things."

A few other boys? he wondered, but wasn't damned fool enough to ask. He wanted to put his arm around her—at least that—but wasn't damned fool enough to try it.

"I'm an electrician," he said, "and I make good wages, but I was married to a white woman and I got child support to pay, even though the child isn't mine. It kind of takes the heart out of you, you know. You want to just give up sometimes. And beat hell out of guys who get insulting and that stuff, you know. But in a new place, out of my ex-wife's lawyer's reach, I'd get to keep my own money and start my own business in four or five years."

"I'm good with computers," she said. "I'd get a job. Tomorrow, we could take this jeep down to where my car is parked and travel together from there." She looked straight at him, the campfire flames a steady glow in her eyes. "I don't mean anything about the future, but I like you, and I owe you. If you wanted, we could pick a city and drive my car there. I haven't much stuff to move."

"If you want even less, you should try divorce."

"I'd have to try marriage first."

She laughed. And he laughed with her.

Would he? If she had asked—hinted, even—he might have gotten the wrong idea, said yes to the wrong thing.

Would she? If he had asked, she'd have said No—or Yes—and it would have all been different.

A pine cone fell in the darkness behind them. And rolled into a fissure holding enough earth. Or came to rest on rock.

# Crazy Horse Morris and an Orange Boat

"Morris, you crazy sonofabitch, you'll drown," Big Dan was yelling, and the other guys yelled something just as his ears split chill water.

To shorten the time he'd have to try to swim, he had dived far out, and for as long as he dared, he swam blind under choppy waves, and sure as hell, when he came up for breath he was right on target, the orange boat bright against green bushes.

Weakening, he forced himself to frog-kick and dog-paddle on, until, arms feeble as fishworms, trailing, he had to collapse, with a last gulp of air, into the dead-man's float, drifting then, and resting until pale light shimmered off gravel bottom.

An orange blur in his eye-corner, he got himself started again, legs kicking pretty good, until knees digging into sand, elbows scrabbling, he could push himself up onto shore, alongside the boat, his half-froze nose sucking in the smells of perfume and pot above a slender footprint.

Maybe some girl had a big boyfriend on top of her, hidden in thick bushes. He'd better get his icy ass out of sight, warm up, then row that pretty orange boat back to his buddies before any more footprints got made in this sand.

After stumbling along a shallow, murky, brush-lined creek a few yards from where it flowed into the clear river, he just dropped, flopped over, and lay, head pillowed on backflung arms to keep his long, black, girl-alluring hair out of muck, while sun and the tepid water began to thaw him.

In sky reflected between his thighs, as hawks drifted, as he, himself, had drifted in the shallows, resting to let himself get strong enough to swim ashore. What if I'd drowned, he thought, and all people had to say was, "Wouldn't you know Crazy Horse Morris would get himself killed someday in some crazy way"—swimming to steal a rowboat, to impress some friends he'd probably never see again once he was in the navy.

"Indian kid like you, out here in the boondocks, what chance does he got for a big-bucks job, big car, big house, pretty little squaw, all that good American Dream stuff?—the chance of a snowball in hell, that's what he's got. Waits to be drafted—a year in Vietnam—or a goddamned eternity in a military cemetery, with all the other losers. You don't look like no loser. You got balls. Like old Gee-ron-eemo. Get trained. Learn electronics or something. An easy eight-hour day on one of the finest ships in the world. Better than sweating in the beet fields, huh? Girls in every port. What do you say?"

"I got one girl too goddamned many already, and what I say is, Hell, yes."

"But my mom won't let me go on the pill, and you don't have a rubber," Alice said; but under her shiny graduation robe, her nails were only making little love-bird pecks against his hand.

"Take a chance," he murmured in her sweaty ear. "Columbus did."

Hearing a splash and afraid the orange boat's owners were about to row away, he sat up, and saw a salmon struggling through shallows toward him, the fish over three feet long and as big around as a fire hydrant, but dark, too dark for eating, only a few bright scales left, a huge white blotch spread over flesh already half rotted off its skull. Slamming its tail against mud, it swam a few inches, gills desperately opening and closing, now in air, now in water, the delicate insides and the scummy outside reminding him of a guy who'd skidded his motorbike on parking-lot gravel—mouth gasping, clean blood inside, dirt outside.

The salmon had to keep its gills under water or die—die without having laid any eggs up at the head of this drizzly little stream, where instinct told it its parents' parents' parents had spawned—when the water had been deeper and the logging companies hadn't left it all clogged with silt.

He thought of salmon ceasing to eat once they'd left the ocean and started their spawning migration up a river—appetite clicking off like a goddamned switch when saltwater stopped coming into the gills.

He thought of his arms refusing to move, even when he was about to drown. But his head had come up for air when he, by God, had to have air. He thought of his prick rising. All by itself. At the damndest times. Whether there was a chick around or not.

He wondered why salmon, which had stopped eating everything else, would strike at fish-hook-concealing clusters of their own orange eggs, or at plastic imitations. He'd sometimes thought the salmon were destroying drifting eggs to keep other fish from noticing them and snooping around to gobble up the rest of the eggs hidden under some reef and out of the current. Or maybe the salmon had an instinct for preserving the eggs of their own kind, even if it meant eating loose ones to start them over again.

He thought of the Geography film about South American Indians eating the ashes of their dead, and he thought of his mother's people eating trapped salmon like this one during the so-called Great American Depression. "God's gift, like everything else in this world," his mother had told him, her fat finger marking where the Bible told about manna.

He thought that his mother's people weren't much better than vultures, eating half-rotten fish—and screwing the fish out of a chance to lay their eggs in the streams they'd swum so many miles of ocean and river to reach, and starved and beat the flesh off their bones, just to keep things going—more salmon setting out on the tides, century after century.

If his mother's folks were vultures, his dad's hadn't been exactly eagles. They'd all been farm workers or loggers and could stretch food money by skulking and killing deer on mountains game wardens wouldn't try to climb. A photograph album showed skinny little Indian guys like himself and his dad, about half of them in marine or army uniforms or navy swab-jockey suits, battle ribbons showing that they'd known what you had to kill to get fed.

At least they'd known until they'd got settled down too long, like his own old man, working a dumb-shit university janitor's job all day, boozing half the night, or all night if he'd managed to pick up a slut—poor old bastard, good luck to him—no balling at home, probably, just preaching and more preaching until, like he said, he didn't have to go to church on Sunday, he got more preaching than he needed at home.

Mud clogging delicate, bloody-looking gills, the big salmon again threshed to inch into slightly deeper water.

Easing his rested body upright, Morris made his hands slimy with muck so he wouldn't damage the salmon's remaining scales, then slid the big fish back into the center of the stream. It started swimming, steadily swimming—not to save its life but the life in those eggs carried by its rotting mess of body.

He himself had damned near drowned just to steal a pretty orange boat. Just to show off for a bunch of stupid clowns who called him crazy and didn't give a shit really if he lived or died. He was dumber than that fucking salmon, even if he didn't have some switch in his head making him start to starve to death the minute he got a hard-on.

He thought of Alice, so dumb she'd let him slip it into her without a rubber while parked in a parking lot in daylight right after graduation. Pudgy as she was, he'd only half wanted her—had mostly wanted a story to tell. Her belly would soon be telling a story her knife-packing brothers wouldn't want to hear.

He'd miss the hunting and fishing. He'd miss Big Dan and the other roughnecks who'd been his friends—or his audience anyway—for four years.

Seeing them across the river, their fish lines curving like spider silks, only wind tugging those lines, he walked stealthily through sand toward the boat, which was drifting the arc its chain allowed. Somebody had wrapped a shirt around the chain, to protect a sapling's delicate bark, but roots were washed bare, and when the creek dried up, later this summer, seeds would drop onto hot gravel.

With a rock wedge, he struck the padlock dead center and split it, the sound a shot echoing.

"Hey, you!"

Half hidden by laurel leaves, she was naked from neat little shadowy navel to narrow swim-suit bra—the bra shiny orange just like her boat.

Two dudes' pale faces rose from the bushes, level with her naked, tan stomach. Morris whirled to launch the boat, then saw the fat dude's hairy pale arm reach around the chick's orange haunch and hand the solemn, skinny guy a red-white-and-blue cigarette.

Big Dan started whooping and laughing across the river, and the others joined in, no doubt figuring that their smart-assed buddy Crazy Horse Morris had, at last, got caught. He knew he should untangle the boat chain and shove off, but he had to go on looking at the chick's body, so slender and golden in its two orange pieces of almost nothing.

"Come have a whiff on us," the fat dude invited, sinking out of sight into bushes, his buddy and the chick sinking with him.

Morris loosened but did not completely unknot the chain. He'd gotten a few women out of bars that didn't check for underage, and he figured older chicks liked him OK.

"Don't you smoke?" the fat dude's voice asked, a reefer cloud like a cartoon word balloon rising above leaves.

"Hell, yes, I smoke. Like a hot horse turd on an icy road." Morris strode around a bush, dropped his ass onto their fancy tourist-Indian blanket, took a deep drag, and passed the pot to the chick, who was staring at his tight, wet shorts.

He figured that she was ready for somebody who'd go ape in bed, whether she knew it or not—the two dudes like a lot of others he'd seen, ones who seemed to have to have the weed or the bottle a little too often.

"You see, you don't need to steal our boat," the skinny dude said, not so stoned as his fat friend. "We're anarchists and believe in giving people what they need."

"My buddies dared me to move your boat just for kicks," Morris said. Then, thinking of what the chick would think, he added: "They didn't believe I could swim against all those tons of melting snow the mountains were pouring down."

The skinny dude stared at the chick's eyes, which were still staring at Morris's groin.

"We're artists, the fat dude said after taking another two-for-me, one-for-you puff. "Paint pictures of . . ." He seemed to be looking two inches from his sunburned nose at whatever he painted, but it looked just like slightly smoky air. "Shit," the chick said, grabbing out of turn, but taking a puff so short she might have been on a grass diet.

"Yeah, Jake and me are painters, real painters. We win prizes," the fat dude continued, still staring in front of his nose. "Sue here only paints well enough to pass art courses—along with the fact that she fucks."

"Cow crap," she answered.

"No, she doesn't go down for me and not for Jake, even if she is more or less still married to him," the fat dude said, wobbling and moving the match carefully around whatever he saw in front of him, then almost lighting one side of his dimpled chin before he found the red-and-white-striped end of the next reefer.

"You in high school?" the skinny more-or-less husband named Jake asked, having guessed the worst, the sly bastard, and wanting to be damned sure his more-or-less wife was informed.

"I finished high school," Morris told Jakie boy's sad, sneaky face. He let himself have a deep toke and felt the world mellow a little. "I'm starting a great job next week, after a year of fighting in Vietnam."

"Murderer," the chick damned near shouted.

"It was kill or be killed, Sue. I didn't ask to be sent to Nam." The navy recruiter had called it Nam.

"You could have refused to go."

"I refused," the fat dude said, and the chick let him put his head in her lap, but her look made it perfectly clear that that fat head with its wonderful load of college-course-crammed brain might just as well have been a pet cat. "A year in prison," the fat dude continued slowly. "Beat up. Used like a woman. A draft-resister—the real criminals despised me. I'm putting it all into my art."

"You can put it all up your ass," the chick said, and pushed his head off her lap and onto the blanket beside her orange-steel haunch.

"A ball-cutting bitch like most American women," the fat dude mumbled. "Putting out for some instructor who's got a little influence in New York. But her real kick is sexing-up human-type artists like me and Jake and then turning us off."

"Well, Kid, are we going to steal their boat or stay here listening to bullshit?" the chick demanded.

Sad Jake made a grab for his ex-wife.

Morris kicked the bony chin and damned near busted his bare big toe, but the kick had been hard enough to tumble Jake ass over appetite, only able to yell, as his boat and his wife drifted away, "I'm an anarchist, but, by god, I can still call the cops."

"Hey, old Crazy Horse Morris, bring her here."

"Your ass is sucking wind," he hollered at Dan, and settled in with the oars.

"Some friends you've got," Sue muttered, probably secretly hoping he'd turn the boat and take her over for a gangbang.

"I like your friends, too," he told her. "I especially dig your more-or-less husband's silly remark about running five miles through poison oak and blackberry brambles and calling the cops."

"Yeah, well I left him, Kid."

Because of having to row, he couldn't stare her down. She'd probably thought of that when she'd gotten in up front, where she sat like a queen, all golden tan on an orange cushion in the orange V of the prow, her blond bangs glistening.

And calling him "Kid"—she'd probably decided to turn him off by telling him he was too young, the mean twitch. He'd have to play it cool or lose whatever chance he had.

Turning to row again, he saw Jake's skinny body arc out over the water, just as his own had done, and disappear.

And, just as he had done, the dude stayed under the surface chop, not coming up till he had to, then settling into a steady, mechanical stroke, veering with the current to intersect the course of the boat, the last he'd seen of it before diving.

Old Jake had guts.

"The damned fool, he must really love me, and I guess I love him," the chick said. "I suppose we'd better pick him up, or he'll drown."

"I swam across OK," Morris told her.

"He's no Vietnamese peasant," she said, sounding scared. "His parents are famous artists. It'll be prison for you. Abused like the real criminals. Used like a woman."

"I didn't tell him to jump in," he told her, to bug her a little before turning the boat. "What makes old Jake so sad anyway?"

"Dirty shits like you and me, a whole worldful."

Hearing a splash, he thought she'd fallen overboard, but she had an orange life preserver clutched to her tits, and before he could even get the boat turned, she'd caught Jake's wet black head between her thighs and gone drifting with him to shore.

Seeing their life preserver, bright orange like a whale-sized cluster of fake plastic salmon eggs, floating away in the main current, Morris pulled hard on the oars and landed their boat where they could get it, just by wading the little creek. The stink of the all-but-finished salmon still on his hands when he slipped one of two remaining life preservers over his head, he took a last look, but the big fish had either struggled out of sight on its way to lay eggs, or it was indistinguishable from the glitters of shallow water, doomed to become buzzard food.

Running to beat hell to get up speed, he hugged the life preserver to his heaving chest, jumped far out and dropped, feet first, into the ball-shriveling river.

"Tough beans, old Crazy Horse Morris." Big Dan grabbed his arm and helped him crawl up onto shore. "Lost the boat, lost your bet, and lost the chick."

"But I didn't lose my fucking life," he mumbled.

Big Dan said something, and the others said something.

Morris kept his damned mouth shut. He knew he'd tried to bullshit his way through the world one time too many. Marrying Alice, he'd have kept her brothers from cutting his throat, but he'd have screwed himself and cheated Alice out of maybe marrying somebody who'd love her. And maybe, with him gone, Alice would decide to have an abortion.

Dan and the others had gone on back to catching no fish.

He could tell them they were casting too far upstream from the riffle, but, hell, he'd been telling them for four years, and they still didn't know jack shit about anything. He could bait up his own rod, drift a single salmon egg on a number-twelve hook, and bring in a twisting, fighting rainbow trout. Today would be his last chance. Tomorrow he'd draw his paycheck at the end of his hours in the beet field, sell his car, and the day after tomorrow, he'd report for navy boot camp. He'd never been out of Oregon, but his and his parents' signatures were on a goddamned eagle-decorated document, and soon he'd be in Vietnam. "Pretty whores just old enough to bleed," the recruiter had said. "They bounce like fucking-machines for damned near no money."

Or they put a bullet into your gizzard.

"No fish here," Dan was complaining. "Old Crazy Horse Morris don't know shit from Shinola about finding fish."

"Up yours," he told Dan. But then he thought, What the fuck, it's my last day, and said, "All right, you super-duper all-American sons-of-bitch white guys, I'll show you who knows how to fish."

They were looking at him expectantly, and he knew—and he knew they knew—he'd do what he said, as sure as hell.

# A Farewell on the Way
to War

Short red skirt dramatically rising, the young woman who'd been Lack's seatmate on the airplane bowed over his backpack and, slender hand parting black hair from blue eyes, read, "York—same name as that Iowa actress who makes antiwar speeches and speaks up for Indians. Are you a relative?"

"I not only speak up for Indians, I *am* an Indian," Lack retorted, thirty-eight often drastically fucked-up years old, by God, and from now on going to maintain his identity, no matter what. "The actress is my . . . ex-wife."

"Ex–cellent!" the young woman laughed, glistening tongue tip a pink comma fluttering between pink parentheses. "I'm Fledge—short for Fledgling—and if you're hanging loose in San Francisco, I'll take you to a peace demonstration. Then, if you haven't already got a pad in this city named for peaceful St. Francis, you can crash with me."

Loudspeakers were warning that flights would be delayed due to a bomb threat as Lack and Fledge made their way through a lobby jammed by soldiers—some with battle ribbons and expectant faces, going home, others with firing-range badges and tense faces. There were well-dressed, middle-aged women selling little American flags under a banner demanding that a U.S. army officer convicted of massacring civilians be released. There were clusters of young people with beggars cups and with signs making vague claims for a new religion. Barbered and coiffured passengers were trying to shove through lines of long-haired men and women, whose placards read, "SOME BOMBS AREN'T HOAXES. STOP KILLING CHILDREN!"

At the exit, two shirtless men greeted Fledge with breast-compressing hugs and beard-circumferenced smooches. "My roommates, Fog and Cloud," she said, and both greeted Lack with embarrassingly prolonged embraces, but after they got into the front seat of their old car and passed back a hand-rolled, spit-slicked marijuana cigarette, Lack decided that they were OK.

At the antiwar rally, a roar like that of an Iowa City football crowd sent "Peace Now! Peace Now!" echoing among a university's imitations of ancient Greek temples. Above sirens' shrill warnings and a cop-helicopter's clatter, a Volkswagen van's old engine's backfires echoed like gunshots, and someone shouted that the principal speaker had just arrived, after being delayed by bomb threats at the airport.

"What happens after the speech?" Lack asked Fledge.

Absorbed in inhaling a toke from some guy's red-white-and-blue reefer, she only shook her head, long black hair swinging across jiggling, blue-T-shirt-covered breasts; but Fog or Cloud called back, as he ambled away, "You want to know what's going down? He'll tell us," nodding toward an army go-to-hell cap, just visible above heads encircling a microphone.

"U.S. imperialism." Lack had heard it from university students. Now, a uniformed soldier shouted it to hundreds of cheering people and told them, raising an arm that ended just below the elbow, "We're going to destroy student records to keep the FBI from sending some of you where I lost *this*. MARCH!"

Committed to saving the lives of Americans as young as he had been when he'd volunteered for America's war in Korea, Lack marched, with hundreds of others, toward stone steps guarded by two bears, brass fur ablaze in falling sun, and by men who brandished steel pipes above yellow work helmets. Some protesters climbing a slope to become spectators, Fledge whispered, "We'll need to see which way to run," and, "drastically impractical sandals" slung over wrists, she first set one naked foot sole down onto a chrome bumper, then, short red skirt enticingly rising, crawled on hands and knees to the roof of a car.

Drastically practical combat boots denting clouds reflected in blue automobile paint, Lack climbed after her, flexing metal intensifying the dizziness he already felt after nights of sleep lost while failing to get laid back home and after today's dope.

Low-cut necklines in the crowd below his viewpoint confirmed that "hip chicks" had, as the media put it, "burned their bras" while young men had burned draft cards. Glimpses up the nearby slope revealed that some young women had bared lower curves of buttocks beneath hems of "hot shorts." Some, like Fledge, wore skirts brief as those cheerleaders wore to entertain football fans. Others were garbed in long "granny gowns," prettily printed with petals, unlike the drab gowns Lack's grandmother had worn.

There were men dressed as impeccably as the banker who'd called Lack's Farmers-Union-organizer Dad a Red-talking Redskin, and there were pale-faced men with Indian headbands, Indian necklaces, and knives in Indian-beaded sheaths. Lack imagined ritual scalpings and saw hundreds of black, brown, or blond warrior trophies, combed or wild, spreading a rug from his boots to the Greek temple's gold-pelted guardian bears and yellow-helmeted guardian men.

"So much for our peaceful peace demonstration," Fledge cried, as dozens of automobile hubcaps began sailing, like gracefully gliding frisbees, over the multitude of heads.

Glittering window fragments clattering down onto yellow helmets, middle-aged patriots charged from white stone steps and clubbed young spectators come early to get up front. Latecomers, hearing screams, surged to see and innocently pushed new victims forward over those already fallen. Several protesters continued gleefully sailing hubcaps to break windows, unaware that steel pipes were bludgeoning a path through the crowd, guided by frisbees' lines of flight.

Fledge jumped from the car roof, short red skirt flaring like a parachute above brief, white Bikini panties, and disappeared among people struggling to see what she was fleeing.

A loudspeaker voice and one gunshot echoing off building after building, Lack jumped and, dizzy from marijuana, fell into fragrance of freshly watered lawn, stumbled up into stench of tear-gas, and began running, pounding combat-booted feet against soft earth, running past windows, flashing like lightning in sun.

"This way, Lack? Jack?" echoing, he followed, stoned and confused, seeing, in rows of windows' reflections, his multiplied Indian-skinned self, pursuing pale women.

Fog and Cloud's car speeding away from where they'd parked it, Fledge cried, "Bastards!" Then, blue eyes squinting through tangled black hair into autumn sundown, she asked, "When do you fly to Vietnam?"

Though dimly remembering a high school girl's anger at being a one-night stand, half of his life ago, Lack mumbled, awed by thoughts of death and unable to lie, "Tomorrow morning."

"We'll make the most of it." Fledge murmured without resentment, her young voice motherly with sympathy. "I've always wanted to sleep with an Indian, and I've always wanted to sleep with an older man."

Indian-braided blond heads pillowed between blond women's granny-gowned thighs, Fog and Cloud were sprawled beside a polar-bear-huge white dog, on the floor of a room whose only furniture seemed to be the tiny TV, flickering just beyond glittering toenails.

When Fledge yelled, "Thanks for bugging out and leaving us to walk to a goddamned bus, thanks for nothing," bare toes twiddled TV's "PEACE NOW" roar louder, and Fog or Cloud slurrily articulated, "You're just in time. He's going up there. He's one righteous dude. Going up there, Man. It's the third time we've seen this. It's on every channel. He's a goddamned Jesus Kee-ricet, a going right up those fucking Roman marble steps."

On the television, the one-armed sergeant strode across glittering window fragments, but instead of entering shattered doors his followers had bled trying to reach, he raised a black plastic bullhorn to teeth flashing between bearded lips and, stump-arm pointing, pleaded, command voice tiny on the tiny TV set, "This is a fucking no-win situation. GO BACK!"

Armageddon thunder of gun echoing, the bullhorn fell, and a dark four-leaf-clover shape spread across pale uniform shirt.

In memory's version of an LSD Eden, advertising neon and car lights and traffic lights, between Venetian blinds, painted multicolor tiger stripes on Fog or Cloud's girlfriend's white dog.

Cloud or Fog on all fours, blond-bearded blond head between a goddess's glowing golden thighs, the drug-addled dog heard its mistress's orgasm cry, followed by, "Yes, yes, and you, too. Come! Oh, yes, yes. Come!" Obeying the command, "Come!" the dog slowly stumbled, as wobbly as a gigantic puppy, toward a green, then red, then green traffic-light-lit scrotum dangling, like the previously proffered dope-soaked doughnut.

Startled awake by Cloud or Fog's yelp of pain and a woman's, "BADBAD DOG!" Fledge heard laughter through drug-confusions, and hugging Lack's snickering lips to her sweaty breasts, murmured, "Don't cry, Baby, don't cry, you'll come back, you won't die." Lack fell asleep, hearing her sleepily crooning, "We met on a jet plane, up in the air, we got it together up in the air, we got high together, and down, down, we went down together, down, down, down."

Leaving men, women, and dog, seemingly dead but probably peacefully dreaming, in a tangle of mummy-case-shaped sleeping bags, Fledge drove Lack to catch his dawn flight.

After an airport breakfast, she mumbled happily, "My stick-in-the-mud West Branch, Iowa, friends are stuck in Herbert Hoover's tourist-trap birthplace, and wait'll they hear that I've been getting it on with an Indian who's also a movie star's ex–old man."

She murmured a tearful farewell, tears maybe for the death that might be awaiting Lack in Asia, maybe for a blurred sense of beauty he and she had dreamed and had tried to live.

Over a row of go-to-hell-capped heads of soldiers two decades younger than Lack and five or so years younger than herself, Fledge cried, "I love you, Lack?—Jack?—Mac?—I love you."

Pizza, some drugs, some sex, and a little sleep was all they'd shared, and they'd not exchanged addresses, but Lack compassionately, gratefully, and truthfully called back over his shoulder, into the country he was leaving, maybe not ever to return, "I love you, too, Fledge—Fledgling. I love you, too!"

# Losers and Winners:
# An Ongoing Indian War

A big, bloody fish swinging between them, their blue eyes roving over skin as brown as the smooth surface of the Mississippi, two men swaggered past Irene.

She unclenched one hand from her little boy's stroller and, silver traffic-control button a werewolf-killing bullet, pressed her own reflected fingerprint—the fingerprint, like her poems, like nobody else's in the world—and one individual, one fragile, Indian individual, brought hundreds of tons of powerful, onrushing, American automobile steel to a stop.

Pressing a sun, reflected, gem-size, in an apartment-entrance button, evoked, "Who in Hell, Missouri, U.S.A. is it?" electronics warping to witch-cackle Mary Jane's playfully posturing voice, which an envious male student poet had called "affected."

Trying to sound as don't-give-a-damn self-confident as Mary Jane had urged her to be, in the class they'd both attended until last night, Irene spunkily announced herself as "Irene the Serene," quoting her former Creative Writing instructor—former lover. Then she added, appealing to Mary Jane's sense of irony, "Irene, the banished Cherokee poetry queen, accompanied by an accomplished prince, who is simultaneously learning to walk and to talk."

Sunset street gave in to shadowy stair, and in a burst of light above, Mary Jane, a flame-haired, movie-image goddess, emerged, her raiment black bra and red underpants.

A big white dog tried to lunge past naked legs, but Mary Jane dragged it, its nails clicking on wood, into the apartment and banged an inner door shut.

Climbing backward to ease wheels up steep steps, Irene frantically clutched the stroller with both sweat-slippery hands, when her friend, trying to help, hugged her from behind and pulled, nearly causing her to stumble over a threshold.

"First, I want you to see what I see of the Mississippi," Mary Jane cried, brazen in her underwear in front of a window. "High above! That's the right perspective for a writer, right? Small boats, even canoes, like those of one *banished* woman's Vanishing American forebears—big barges for coal, oil, uranium—whatever the U.S. requires to turn the whole world into an Indian reservation. And my view includes floating gambling casinos, the all-night between-decks lights so bright my binoculars show men and women and men and men and women and women playing their own games of chance. You'd be surprised. Or maybe you wouldn't be. I'll know when I know you better."

Red-and-white bobbers swinging as the fish had swung, in the rhythm of the swaggering men, long fish poles were toothpick-tiny in the distance. Looking across brown water in the direction from which the men had come, Irene saw one of the gambling boats Mary Jane had mentioned. The anchored boat was as big as a department store, its decks empty except for one white-jacketed, white-haired black man, wiping railings—his polishing, and sundown, making them glow as bright as the day they'd been forged.

Irene knew that "a gambling boat, as big as a department store" might have won praise from her professor, who had seemed the ideal man she'd dreamed since girlhood, someone who'd help her find meaning in existence. He'd scorned her as "too bookish to be a writer," and she could no longer share poems Fridays—Friday, named for Freya, goddess of love, marriage, and fecundity, Irene remembered, and also the queen of the Valkyries, Viking goddesses, who were warriors like some of Irene's own Cherokee foremothers.

"Usually words *mean,* and it takes a genius, like e. e. cummings, to make them *not* mean, and thus to remind us, in this age of verbal sprawl, that words aren't life, no matter what we've been told. Yes, *told!* From kindergarten to the final graduation, which only worms attend. Call me Clint. I'm not a professor, I'm a poet—a poet who makes a living from teaching."

Clint had opened class by opening two bottles of red wine and saying, "A senator's wife destroyed some champagne to launch the destroyer on which I killed time, with books, and —with guns—people. This tour of duty is about creating, not destroying, and our craft will be one once skippered by an ex-warrior named Shakes–Spear."

Clint's lovemaking had been savage, Irene's response so wild she hadn't heard her little boy crying for her. Now, under Mary Jane's shrewd, perceptive gaze, she only hoped that her blush would seem to be due to summer heat.

"Time for today's ration of grog, as they are said to have said in the Limey navy," laughed Mary Jane—whose "dippy hippie" parents had named her for marijuana. "And, Irene the Serene, you should calm your audibly beseeching child by letting him exercise his ambulatory accomplishments."

Moving a chair to fence off the electric-fan blades, Irene lifted her restless little boy out of the stroller and freed him to run, as Mary Jane had proposed.

Mary Jane might be all that Irene would have left from Creative Writing. Raymond Bearkiller, a quietly intelligent Cheyenne, had twice shared beer and conversation, but after her after-class get-together with Clint, Raymond had not asked her out again.

"Because I'm married, ours must remain a one-night fulfillment, and yours must remain a one-term try at writing," Clint had decided, staring at stretch marks around her navel, his one recognition that she was the mother of the child whose cries he'd heard and—less carried away than herself—had called to her attention. "You're shy, Irene, like most of the Indian women I've taught. Your bookishness protects your vulnerability, but you're too fragile to compete with career poets."

Not fragile at all, Mary Jane swung one bare leg and blocked her snarling dog while elbowing the kitchen door shut behind her, all without spilling drinks brimming and shimmering on a huge tray that glowed like a bronze shield.

Mary Jane's, "Cheers," was the same "Briticism" Clint had offered as a farewell toast in Irene's bedroom.

Writing amusingly of women who emerged from breakups more in harmony with themselves and with the universe, Mary Jane's experiences had undoubtedly been a lot more interesting than Irene's only experience, before Clint. "Forget that one, that one won't see you through," Irene's preacher father had counseled, as he'd counseled throughout Irene's high school years and halfway through her year in college. "See me *through* what, *to* what?" Irene had wanted to know; but her timid Cherokee mother, who considered herself a blessed helpmeet to a white missionary husband, had answered, "Obey your father."

When Irene had finally obeyed derisive girlfriends' counseling and her own urges, memory of a sex-education class had been as sketchy as her memory of every class that was not literature. Her child's father dumping her and resuming his sex life with others, she had begged her mother and father for help in raising their grandchild; but her father had only offered to arrange for adoption. Carrots, olives, and radishes, as colorful as candies, drew Irene's little boy, running and stumbling, and the gin already taking effect, Irene was almost too slow in getting an arm between soft cheek and the bronze tray's sharp edge. After scraping peppery meat into her own mouth, she gave her son the bare cracker, and as generous as he'd often been with playmates in public parks, he ran to try to feed a pigeon, butter-covered fingers smearing Mary Jane's high window.

The white-uniformed, white-haired black man was still polishing already glowing railings of the big gambling boat's top deck, and Irene thought that whatever might happen between couples up on that deck tonight, she'd be lying in her own lonely sweat and getting up each time her teething little one's gums hurt.

"It's Saturday," she heard herself say aloud—the gin, she knew—but like a child unable to keep its tongue from wiggling a loose tooth, she went on: "You were in class last night?"

"Well, yes," Mary Jane responded, getting to her feet and moving to spread her bare legs in front of the fan. "But next term I'll find a better instructor."

"Better than Clint?"

"Fuck, yes!" Mary Jane laughed, her ironic laughter always the start of one of her classroom diatribes. "He's only had one book published. He's almost middle-aged. And he is *so-o* retro. In a stormy sea of female voices protesting centuries of injustice, his life preserver is limp, its air the hot air of his pitiful boasts about cannonading Asian fishermen and feeling mildly guilty while enjoying mistreating half-starved women in port. He romanticizes trivial domestic infidelities as fertility rituals, but shit! no woman needs a surveillance camera under the toilet seat to know that an altar a cunt is not."

"Did Clint ever . . . ?" Irene heard a delicate clicking against glass, the pigeon's beak or small fingernails, and she hurried on as if her little boy might come toddling back, able to understand what his mother was asking her poised friend—able to understand what had gone on in his mother's bed while he'd chewed his thumb bloody to ease sore gums. "Did Clint . . . ?"

"I slept with him," Mary Jane answered. "Who didn't? Sure he's married, but that's his problem."

"For only one night?" Irene persisted, not sure of why she needed to know.

"One night when I didn't have anything better to do," Mary Jane laughed. "That was just after I moved here, among the loading docks, where rent is cheap enough for a divorced, unemployed woman dedicated to writing—and where the men I meet in bars are as real as the fish they hook, gut, and eat—as strong as the river. Clint, who probably lives in a huge house among huge houses on a hill, won my final vestige of emotional virginity by telling me he felt my poems were starting to get the brute courage he says a writer needs and most women lack—a courage he got in war, he claims, but when my jealous dog jumped onto the bed, it scared Clint's pants off. Figuratively. Literally, they were already as off as pants can get."

Avoiding Mary Jane's inquisitive gaze, Irene turned and found her son still at the window. His pretty bird had flown, but encircled by darkening, gleaming bronze water, the gambling boat's lights were as colorful as candies on a tray.

When Mary Jane cried, "I see your glass is ready for a refill," Irene heard herself say, "Why not?"

"Why the hell not?" Mary Jane echoed, lifting the tinkling ice of their drinks and leaving the heavy tray. "And take off that hot dress. Wear what your Indian people wore, the never-out-of-style air, and welcome the seductively gentle breath of my fan."

Her sophisticated friend cool and uninhibited in underwear this whole while—and seemingly right at home in a world of her own words, own flesh—Irene thought, "Why not? Why the hell not?" But she heard her son babbling, and with only one button undone, she walked to the window, her legs—wobbly from alcohol—feeling as unreliable as her child's little legs.

"Owie," was what he was murmuring, using the term his babysitter had used for his thumb, bloodied by teething, and he was pointing toward the old black man's polishing rag, which the gambling boat's fire-exit light had turned as red as a bloody fish.

Hearing Mary Jane kick the kitchen door open, Irene hurried back to the tray table, fumbling free a second button, and, her child following, the white dog lunged past Mary Jane's bare legs toward the sound of little, stumbling feet.

Irene moved to block the snarling beast, and when it veered to get around her, she snatched up and swung the drinks tray, feeling, while off-balance she fell amid scattering veggies, heavy bronze thud against skull.

"You vicious, Indian bitch!" Mary Jane screamed. "You've killed my dog!" But Irene, crawling across the white body to soothe her frightened child, felt the stunned dog's lungs still pumping fast from its run to attack.

The floating gambling casino, brightly lit like a department store, was reflected as small as a bathtub toy in the curve of the street-crossing button. For the second time in that day's minuscule fraction of eternity, Irene's fingerprint found its own—headlight-lit, now—reflection, like nobody else's in the world, and hundreds of tons of powerful, onrushing, American automobile steel stopped.

Downriver, a few blocks past where long fish poles' red-and-white bobbers had disappeared, Irene wheeled her little boy into one of the inexpensive "Eats" places, which she'd always avoided after dark, till now. A man, with tattooed mermaids swimming hair as thick as seaweed on his forearms, patted the head of her drowsy child, then served fish and chips. Between swallows, she fed her little one well-chewed mouthfuls; then, she thanked the man, paid him, tipped him, and left him to wash the dishes.

Back in her hot apartment, her son sung to sleep, she checked the answering machine. Someone had called, but had left only line static as message.

Maybe Mary Jane wanted to apologize and renew her dinner invitation, Irene thought, and didn't care. Maybe Clint was offering champagne on the dark top deck of a destroyer and inviting his "banished and vanished redskin" onto his craft for another night's tour of duty.

Shy, bookish, fragile Irene the Serene would respond as a Cherokee Warrior Woman. She would canoe upstream, against the current. Her soprano thunder, "That one won't see you through from bridal chamber to funeral parlor," would echo from shore to shore—across the Great Divide—from America the Beautiful's Sea to Shining Sea.

Finding last term's class list, Irene phoned the only person likely to have left static on her answering machine.

"Irene, the not so serene, worried that we might lose touch," she offered.

"Raymond—Beerkiller here, killer of beers, and I was hoping we could kill one or two after class last night, but Soul Killer Clint said you'd dropped out. I tried to call earlier."

"And didn't leave a message."

"Sorry—electronic voices—calling in helicopter gunship strikes, artillery, napalm—my problem. Could we talk across a table somewhere?"

Remembering Mary Jane's story, "Ms. Custer's One Night Stand," Irene thought that she and Ms. Custer's "laughably shy, sun-worshiper, whose eyes were black suns in dusky-sky skin," might have some things to talk about—or some things to *not* talk about. Since it'd be too late to find a sitter for her son, would Raymond like to come over, but just for one beer?

He asked—regretfully, she thought—"Would tomorrow night be better?" and she said, regretfully, gratefully, and hopefully, "Yes."

# A Monster Mosquito Seeking Blood

His day begun with seven sacred, pine-scented breaths, Ames heard a tent flap unzip, and heard yesterday's cowgirl-costumed actress urging her huge, white-cowboy-hatted husband, "Shoot him! He's so young, and his back's all scarred, from some savage ceremony. Shoot him!" Her tone said that she'd liked what she'd said, and she said it once more: "Shoot him!"

Ames continued walking until he reached the canyon edge's sheer drop. There, although a camcorder was buzzing like a monster mosquito seeking blood, he began his prayers. "Thank you, Great Spirit, for my small part in the immensity, the power, the glory, and the beauty of Creation." With tents of sleeping tourists nearby, his words were silent, as they'd had to be last year when sound might have guided a sniper's bullet.

"Great Spirit of the Earth, in which my people lie and from which growth comes, thank you for the good things which have come to us from the earth."

Ames's mother cut her little helper a slice of seed potato, its white ribboned by blood from her chapped hand.

While Ames's father drove the horses, Ames perched on the jolting wagon's heaped oats and poured bucketful after bucketful into the planter, which whirled pale seeds out over black earth, to grow and provide food for hogs that would be butchered and eaten in winter.

"Now, while his head's still bowed, with that long hair shining like black sun rays! Let me. I know what I want. Oh, yes, I *do* know what I want. And push that button that brings him right up close. Quick! Before he moves. Let me shoot."

Ames's big brother, a cock pheasant's ancestral Asian-jungle-camouflage feathers red-gold against white clouds—four years before he was killed in Vietnam—let Ames, then twelve, shoot, to take for the first time his family's meat.

"Please bless my parents and brother in the Spirit Land and keep them well and let them know that I love them."

Ames continued his prayers: to the Spirit of day's fiery beginning, to the Spirit of the Pole Star's snow-crystal glitter, to the Spirit of day's end's slowly fading glow, and to the Spirit of warm southern winds' life-sustaining rain—rain frozen into this mountain's highest slope's slowly melting glacier, melt become lake, become river, plunging from canyon rim and flowing, through green, all the way to ocean's white, whale-shape clouds.

"Thank you, Great Spirit of this Holy Beautiful Place, for the beauty, surrounding—" last night's new snow, on peaks, crimson in dawn, curved daytime moon the dip of a pale canoe paddle in ice-floe-flecked sky—"and help me, please, to live this day in beauty."

Seven final sacred breaths taken and returned into earth's great sea of air, Ames closed his eyes and let himself feel the lives of ancestors, renewed in his twenty-two-year-old flesh and mind.

The camcorder couple's tent was shaking, as if from a little wind within, and silhouetted through blue nylon, the woman was on all fours, her cowboy-hatted husband on his knees behind her, their come cries awakening the sleepy voices of other tourists, in neighboring tents.

Ames stared down at smog, diminished by distance to a jellyfish, its minuscule tentacles dangling over barnacle clusters of factories. Still, in this mountain's vast shade, Ames's people's reservation houses were smaller than books on Ames's college library's shelves. The library itself was a reservation, Ames thought. In it lived stories—of this world and the next—forebears' tongues moving again, shaping a heritage for Ames's generation and for those yet to be born. A small part of the Athabascan people's conquest of land from the Arctic Circle to Central America, his tribe's history was abundant water and year-round sun, the fields so fertile they'd become the food supply for every passing army and become, now, huge agribusiness corporations' domain.

Ames's college's library made possible learning the past time and feeling timelessness. It made possible freedom from meaningless existence, freedom from meaningless death, and freedom from unemployment, hunger, alcoholism, and hopelessness. Having recognized that he was more intelligent than most people and that learning must be his Spirit Path, Ames had enlisted in the marines, and had killed, to be able to afford an education. Final exams soon, the library was where he needed to be, not here, tolerating the racist camcorder couple's sex quirks.

"Ames, if you don't guide these tourists for your cousin, nobody will hire him when he's not sick."

Sick from drinking every cent of army disability money again, Ames had thought. But, over the electronic moaning of telephone wire, he had heard the sobs of children as hungry as he had been before his dad had made Alcoholics Anonymous his Medicine Path and had used his war veteran's entitlement to get a loan and buy a small farm.

Hearing the tourism-office man state that their guide knew about his people's ancient rock carvings, a young woman, waiting with others inside the touring company's van, had moved into the front seat and introduced herself as Jean. While Ames had driven to where they would begin their climb up the mountain, he'd answered Jean's questions, as professors had answered his, describing a sun whose rays were like arms, reaching to meet the raised arms of worshipers. He had told all he knew from one year's study, but, standing in front of the Sacred Wall's carved sun and carved worshipers, Jean had been attentive while he'd repeated himself for the others.

Dusty and sweaty from a steep, two-hour climb, their group had joined a dozen men and women from other camps in the tourism brochure's "secluded nude bathing option."

The camcorder lens trailing women as they emerged from the lake, Jean had clothed her breasts in glittering ripples, then asked Ames to bring the swimsuit hung on her tent. His hand warming under her armpit, he'd steadied her while she'd floated and tugged wet cloth up submerged legs.

The camcorder wife had used her body—bare except for her red cowgirl neckerchief—to shield her husband's camcorder from view while he—naked except for his white cowboy hat—had filmed young women. When some of them had noticed and objected, the wife had laughed, "'It's just light on skin,' he says, 'and light belongs to everyone.' He thinks he's whatever film director said that, but to me, he's a big, handsome cowboy actor. Anyway, he's only practicing filming. The camcorder is empty. He used the last film on those toothpick-legged rock-cartoon women."

Jean had swum a suit out to the gray-haired woman Ames had thought Jean's mother, until Jean had corrected him: "We're a couple, but probably not for long," adding, looking toward the camcorder pair, "To bigots, I'm a pariah—like a half-breed Indian, maybe—because I date both women and men."

"Half-breed" Ames had understood, though his dark complexion spared him the label that many, his light-skinned cousin among them, had to endure. About "a couple" he'd been uncertain. Other soldiers had despised more sensitive men as "Queers," but had snickered and goosed one another while waiting their turn at raping women. The girl he'd loved lost to another man, prostitutes had been Ames's illusory revenge for a time, and then his solace. "A couple, but probably not for long," could have applied to him and his girlfriend, this past year, at college.

Hours after sundown, a final history chapter read, Ames had turned off his flashlight, and from the darkness over him, Jean had murmured, "I wish I could sleep, as you do, under the stars. I wish I could wake up seeing the dawn."

"You could, Jean," he had cried into the darkness, the unknown, the unknowable, hearing in the yearning of his voice the unsaid, You could lie with me, Jean, Jean, Jean, our sleeping bags zipped together, your body warming my body, my body warming yours, Jean, making love or talking as we talked while climbing the trail, Jean, sharing our college study as if it were a childhood in which we had grown up together, knowing things only we knew.

Because he might soon be killed, his girl, during two years of high school, had opened to him, her body and all she had felt she might become. Eighteen, inexperienced and selfish, he'd taken less, far less, than she'd had to give, as he'd realized when she had written from Dartmouth, "We made no promises."

"Let's come here sometime, just the two of us," Jean had said, pale, slender feet moving away into the dark.

"Don't be offended by our shooting you while you were at prayer or whatever just now," the camcorder woman whispered, warming her hands over the breakfast fire, which Ames had laid on last night's ashes. "My husband's one of the Senate Armed Force's Committee Chairman's speechwriters, and he only shares his amateur travelogues with respectable clients—legislators, industrialists, and top-ranking military men. This was our first chance to catch a full-blood doing something traditional."

"I'm dark thanks to some black soldier's no doubt unwilling part in Manifest Destiny," Ames told her angrily, imagining her "respectable" men ogling women emerging, naked, from the shimmering lake, his shrapnel-scarred back explained as due to a "savage ritual"—bodies, bloody on millions of TV screens, explained as "acceptable losses."

"Anyway," he told the camcorder woman, "all the film had been used on those 'toothpick-legged rock-cartoon' women, right?"

She laughed. "People never believe the camcorder is empty, but to avoid trouble, they pretend to accept what I've said. Everyone pretends. All of us tourists are pretending we're Native Americans, swimming naked, cooking our wretched meals over burning wood, sleeping in nylon tepees. It's no fun just being yourself. Even children pretend.

They pretend to be doctors and nurses so they can mess around with each other. They pretend to be cops and robbers, cowboys and Indians, space heroes and aliens, GI's and gooks—you name it. Actors help people pretend to live exciting lives. I should know. I struggled on stage until I married and moved into the big time, helping my husband help politicians pretend to be what voters want them to be. With so many against the war, my husband has to write each of the Armed Services Committee chairman's speeches as if it were the Gettysburg Address, and that means he has to pretend to be what no public-relations man will ever be, a statesman as eloquent as Abe Lincoln.

"'Dreaming your ancestors helps you to become your best self.' That's what you said at the end of yesterday's charmingly, youthfully sincere, and slightly pompous, lecture. You were probably pretending you were whatever professor taught you, but your mind wasn't on those toothpick-legged women a thousand years gone into the dust beneath our hiking boots, your mind was on that young thing you thought was sexy, and now she's inside her tent, pretending the woman with her is a man. Pretending just for fun is as American as the Thanksgiving turkey, but pretending as a step toward changing your life, that's where pretending becomes creative imagination—becomes, maybe, what you called the Medicine Dream. With thousands of rioting blacks providing pressure, there are opportunities for a young, dark-skinned man. I'm in a position to know what those opportunities are, and I can help. I've been in your situation. There were no Equal Opportunity breaks for women when I was an economically disadvantaged student. I'm much more intelligent than my husband, but he has the fantastic job. I have him, such as he is, and what he is isn't worth portraying in a B movie or even in one of his own camcorder skits.

"You seem as intelligent as I am, and if you could pretend I'm the age I was a few years back, you'd find me desirable. Yesterday you saw me without a stitch of clothes, and I saw that you were not displeased. Imagine my mature curves in lingerie that cost more than your college tuition. Dinner, drinks, and a motel not far from here—everything at my expense, of course—and some of the cash an ambitious college student like yourself always needs—and deserves. The young woman you find so sexy might like to join you and me. Give my suggestions some thought. With enough financial incentive, you could pretend that the camcorder is empty, right?"

It'll be empty, all right, Ames thought, totally empty, and answered the way he usually answered the occasional propositions of tourist women, and men, by saying nothing.

While the group emerged from a night on thin pads inside cramped tents, ate day-old doughnuts and drank coffee tasting of smoke, Ames walked to the canyon's edge, his gaze following eons-extinct volcanoes' snow's melting into lake, from which the river flowed, irrigating pastures all the way to ocean. Ames's brother had died and Ames himself had almost bled to death on the other side of that ocean, and though heavy footsteps were coming up behind him, he finished, aloud, a final prayer: "Great Spirit, please help me to live well enough and long enough to fulfill my destiny."

"Hey, man, this lens brings her as close as you are to me."

Over ancestors' voices crying in wind, rising against steep canyon stone, the camcorder buzzed like a monster mosquito—telephoto lens aimed where a toilet had been dug, to drain away from the lake. The toilet had no walls, but, distant from other campers, anyone perched on the board seat seemed as small as a figure carved into rock a thousand years ago.

"This will complete the skit of her, so enticingly outraged and ordering you to bring her swimsuit yesterday," the camcorder man chuckled. "I like you, and what's even more important in these triangular situations, my wife likes you. Want to learn to be a film maker? There's a market for it. Here. But you'll be holding a month's pay, so keep a damned good grip on the strap. When our snooty goddess stands and starts to pull her pants up, just push that red button and shoot."

"This makes me think of the red nuclear button your president or some other enemy might be pushing right now," Ames said, and let the camcorder drop five hundred feet onto rocks.

Hands reaching, belatedly trying to catch his toy, the big man muttered, "Your guide job just slipped from your clumsy fingers, you red nigger son of a bitch, and your tour company will be buying me a new camcorder." Ames knew that his cousin's employers' signup forms freed them from responsibility in case of accidents," but—a swarm of tiny suns reflecting off shattered lens, five hundred feet below the scuffed toes of his old combat boots—he said, "We can find your plaything on our way down."

"Find? You know damned well it's wrecked!"

"You must carry it to a trash can so as not to pollute. The speeches you write for your senator claim that he respects our environment, and he's been supplying Vietnam with fertilizer."

"Speeches? Oh, so my bitch wife has been telling you that story, has she? Don't come on all ironic with me, college boy. I may sell used cars for a living, but I'm a hell of a lot better with words than you are."

Ames turning his back—which white civilization had savagely and unceremoniously scarred—the flirtatious tourist wife's huge husband cried after him, "And don't pretend this is about politics. It's about that little, black-haired bi-sex bitch, isn't it?"

The distant tourism town's rows of windows the gleams of dimes in a cash-register tray, the reservation's renovated army barracks as tiny as museum-diorama tepees, Ames said, "It's about hate." And, he thought, it's about love—something, maybe love, beginning—ancestors' war cries and serenades in the canyon wind.

# A Way Home

Struggling to get his one good eye down close enough to read his connecting flight's gate number and still keep his balance on crutches, Whippoorwill Willis regretted drinking wine, which a luxury-class passenger had sent back to men in uniform—a bounty, like the whiskey that colonists were paid for my Cherokee people's scalps, Whipp thought, his mind moving on a few days to when he'd again be studying American history and maybe be able to do what an army psychologist had urged him to do, find an acceptable place in his life for anger—that place like a goddamned Indian reservation, why the hell not, an anger reservation—better than some military loony bin.

Ann, a future classmate who'd shared his wine on the flight from Japan, caught up with him, her knuckles white with the strain of carrying both his and her bags. "Our gate is a long way," she said, "but here comes help."

"Watch where the hell you're going!" a man shouted, and the young woman bringing a wheelchair shouted back, "I'm watching. I'm watching."

"Hurry, please, or we'll miss our next flight," Ann told the young woman, who'd already hurried in turning the chair and had nearly sideswiped someone's luggage cart.

"We'll make it, we'll make it," the wheelchair woman said cheerily as Whipp dropped into the canvas seat. When she repeated, "We'll make it, we'll make it," grinning past her own blue-uniformed shoulder while kneeling to flop down silver footrests, Whipp recognized that she was . . . "mentally challenged" as people said now—"goofy" as good as it got in the town where he'd grown up. "Mentally Challenged" helps "Physically Challenged," he thought. "Goofy helps crippled redskin." But he wondered about "helps" when the whirling wheelchair made Ann jump to one side.

An older woman not so nimble, Whipp's cast-encased foot tangled in her suitcase strap, twisted free and bounced, hurting like hell, along concrete, past veering luggage carts, until Ann caught up, lifted the bullet-shattered foot, and eased it down beside his other foot.

"I know the gate. I know the gate," the challenged woman said heedlessly. "We'll make it. We'll make it."

"Look out!" Whipp cried as the wheelchair overtook and just missed a well-dressed man, whose angry yell alerted an Asian couple to part, the map they'd been sharing ripping between them, a big black-lettered "San" and blue bay flapping past Whipp's left eye, "Francisco" and land vanishing on his blind side.

"Be careful, please." In Ann's voice, Whipp heard the same sympathy he'd heard when she had seen his crutches and his bandaged eye.

Gratitude brought alive the boy he had been, a boy whose Indian mother had died young, a boy whose white father had spent more time in the tavern than he'd spent at home. A neighbor woman, her own children grown, had fed the motherless boy more than she could spare, given him an Indian name, Whippoorwill, and told stories that had created a role model, a father figure, a hero, Chief John Ross, Guwisguwi, a mixed-blood who'd sacrificed his wealth and risked his life to do what he could for his Cherokee people.

"Sorry! SorrySorrySorry!" the mentally challenged attendant chanted, again and again, as she jostled past anyone slower than her speeding chair. "Sorry 'bout that," Whipp's buddies had mouthed, to joke away the killing they had had to do.

Whipp was glad an airline had hired the mentally deficient young woman and given her a chance to live as normally as possible, just as he, a one-eyed and crippled Indian, was getting some government assistance for college—getting a chance.

"Out, out! Out of Vietnam!" pursuing the careening wheelchair, the mentally challenged young woman chanted, "Out, out! Out of the way! Out, out! Out of the way! Sorry. Sorry. Sorree-ee. We'll get there. We'll get there! I know where I'm going. They told me and told me. I know where I'm going. Out, out, out of the way!"

"Watch out! Watch out!" Whipp began chanting, and then, because it didn't matter as long as he was alerting people ahead, he chanted, as he'd chanted for a year before the army got him, "Out, Out! Out of Vietnam," and chanted, for variety and irony, "Out, Out of Indian Land." To encourage his wheelchair attendant, he chanted, "Great, great, you are doing great," and hurrying along beside them, Ann joined in, "Great! Great!"

"It's my first day on the job," the young woman said, and an elevator's doors ahead slowly closing, she shouted, "Hold it! Hold it!" until someone pressed a button to let the wheelchair jostle, between hastily dodging passengers, and jolt Whipp's foot against a wall. He'd had time to bend his knee, and the hurt was slight, but leaning over to reach the wheelchair's brake, the attendant fell across him and twisted his foot so hard, he screamed.

"Sorree," the challenged young woman was sobbing as Ann lifted her off Will's foot.

"It didn't hurt," Whipp mumbled, mind set against pain, "didn't hurt, didn't hurt."

The elevator emptying, Ann called back, "I'll hold the plane," and awkwardly ran, bags bumping against bare legs, bare shoulders glowing as black hair lifted in wind so strong it nearly blew away the money that Whipp was trying to extricate from a shirt pocket while balancing uncertainly on crutches.

"I got you here, I got you here!" the wheelchair operator laughed. "You did great. You did just great," Whipp chanted, and pressed a bill into her sweaty hand, only noticing after she'd sped away that the Japanese bill he'd grabbed was so small it was as worthless as his pity.

"Hand me up your crutches," a blue-uniformed man yelled from the top of the airplane stairs, "and use both hands on the railings."

Whipp did what medics had trained him to do, gave Ann one crutch, grabbed one rope railing with one hand and used the second crutch to bear his weight while swinging his good foot up onto the first step, but the uniformed man commanded, "Give your wife your other crutch. Both hands on the railings! Both hands on the railings!"

"Don't yell at me!" Whipp yelled, "or I'll shove a crutch up your ass so far it'll come out your hairy nostril!"

Rage fading as the attendant backed into shadow, Whipp mumbled, "Sorry, must be the wine," embarrassed, until Ann laughed, "Good wine. Thanks for sharing."

"I love you," he shouted over the roaring of the goddamned engines.

"Make love, not war," Ann shouted up into sun blazing off metal. Her black hair blown back from blue eyes and gleaming grin as she climbed to join him, he felt immense joy. His mind was functioning OK. Soon he would be able to walk on both feet. One eye would, in time, be nearly as good as new, the other better than no eye at all. And he felt he'd begun to get to know a woman with whom he might share some life.

# Some Indian Wars,
# Some Wounds

Eighteen and strong, I had humped forty pounds of gear forty miles and completed training for battle, but noting a slightly erratic heartbeat, already recorded from previous exams, the medical captain shook his head. "A month ago, I'd have sent you overseas, and it'd of been a bullet that killed you, not a heart attack. I've worked on an Indian reservation and seen you people take advantage. Now the war's damned near ended you might be costing our government a disability pension for a few days of combat."

As temporary duty while awaiting a medical discharge, I was assigned to guard the post gate, checking passes of troops who'd been in town, drinking and getting laid or enjoying a final bar-room battle before getting out of the army and going home.

Because one gate guard had been mobbed by drunks and sent to the hospital, my orders were to wait for troops to get off a bus, line up, and show their passes. A .45 revolver holstered on my belt, I wasn't afraid of unarmed men—who were, anyway, soldiers of my own army—but when several soldiers shoved three fist-swinging paratroops off a bus and the bus sped away, its occupants' passes unchecked, I started for the glassed guard cubicle to phone a report.

"Hey, dipshit!"

I kept on going.

"It's colder'n a witch's tit. We're coming in."

The guard cubicle without a lock, and anyway only walled with glass, I called back, "Welcome," swung the door wide open, and was dialing when a karate chop drove the phone to splinter into black plastic shards against the floor. Faking calm, I demanded, "What the hell was that about?"

The biggest of the three, a sergeant, said, "We wait for the next goddamned bus, then get to hell on back to the goddamned barracks and get some sleep and get out of the goddamned army tomorrow without any shit hitting the fan. You understand me? You getting the goddamned message, fuckhead?"

"I understand you, buddy," I told him. "You want the same damned thing I want, buddy, right down to getting out of the goddamned army." He wore more battle ribbons than I'd dreamed of as a kid. I thought I understood his contempt for a guy who'd never been in combat, but when he said, "I ain't no buddy to no dago!" I understood more than I wanted to understand, having been despised back home as the supposed son of some Italian immigrated to build railroads, bridges, and cities.

The busload of soldiers, with their passes unchecked, had had time to reach the guardhouse; but there was no sound of any military police vehicle, only wind off the Mississippi, which my Cherokee ancestors had been forced to cross, midwinter, on the death march called the Trail of Tears. To have run all the way to the guardhouse, leaving the gate unguarded, would have been a logical decision, but I was as deranged as the three drunks. I'd lost a girl I'd hoped to marry. The enemy had killed my two brothers. I'd enlisted, wanting revenge and ready to die. Then, I'd been accused of trying to cheat the government out of a pension. Though feeling my own and my Cherokee people's humiliation, I decided to wait and hope that soon the next bus would come, and the three drunks could stagger on board. They'd go home, and I'd go home, to live among countrymen for whom the war was just exciting television footage, with patriotic, military music and a voice as hypnotic as that of a sports announcer narrating. There'd be parades, the firing of rifles in salute, the yearly tears on a designated day, the sacrifice of wilting flowers, and twenty years, or sooner, there'd be more patriotic speeches, more exciting television.

Since gate guards weren't allowed to sit, and thus there were no chairs, the sergeant helped one sloshed buddy to lie on the narrow desk, shiny boots dangling.

The other mumbled, "Take a piss," and managed to stumble through the door, prop against a gatepost and get his pecker out in time. Smell drifting in on cold wind recalling a need of his own, the drunk the sergeant had tried to befriend rolled half off the desk, propped against it, then staggered out to lean against the nearest section of cyclone fence, which separated army base from forest.

"This place is starting to smell like a goddamned latrine," I said, and keeping a grip on my holstered gun, sidled past the big sergeant.

The drunk who'd stayed upright by propping against the gatepost had by now staggered almost out of the light, and he was pointing toward a small black and white animal, coming, lurching as if as drunk as himself, toward him—"Kitty, Kitty, Kitty, Pussy, Pussy, Pussy" his understanding.

"That skunk's got rabies," the ex-sergeant yelled at his friend, then yelled at me, "Give me the pistol, dipshit, you probably couldn't hit a bull in the ass with a bass fiddle."

"Skunk," the staggering man giggled. "Drunk as a skunk. You bet. Drunk as a fucking skunk. Here pussy pussy."

All wobbly, it might have rabies, even though late winter wasn't the season.

I drew my weapon, and remembering my war veteran Dad's telling me a double-action revolver was better used single-action, so as not to risk jerking off target, I thumbed the hammer back. Front sight gleaming against dark fur below glittering eyes, the big gun reared up in my hand, and, shot echoing off distant flood levees, the small black-and-white body galvanized, tail up, ready to spray, then collapsed.

"Oh, pussy," the innocently unaware drunk mumbled and, one hand out, urgent to pet, staggered toward the little corpse.

When, grabbing the guy's overcoat collar with one hand and, with the other hand, the half belt in back, the sergeant shoved him into the guard cubicle, I saw my second chance to run; but I shoved a replacement cartridge into the cylinder and strode like a man, by God, like a man, out of the ball-shriveling wind and into the not warm but not quite so cold space that was mine, by God, mine.

"We accept that you expended the first cartridge on an animal you thought rabid, but your second shot—what were you thinking before you pulled that trigger?" the snotty Provost Marshal Office captain asked. I didn't tell him that a real dogface, grunt, ordinary soldier—like me, goddamn it, *like me*—would have said, "*squeezed* the trigger," not "*pulled* the trigger," a pull likely to jerk the gun out of aim. I did what my mother had told me I must always do: I told the truth. What was I thinking? "Nothing," I told the man who might send me to prison. "Nothing."

"Hey, you dipshit dago, we need more heat in here," the drunken sergeant ordered.

"You want more heat, you button your goddamned coat," I said, "and I'm not Italian, I'm Indian."

The feeblest drunk was again sprawled across my desk, an arm pillowing his head, his dangling paratroop boots shinier from being pissed on. He was shivering, the overcoat he'd tried to spread for a blanket twisted around his waist. Maybe intending to soften the defiant speech I'd made, I jerked the coat higher—and a half-full bottle flipped from a pocket.

The time I lost in trying to catch the gleaming whiskey mid-air was the time I should have used to get the hell away.

Hearing his bottle shatter, the guy on the table sleepily mumbled, "And another redskin bit the dust." But driven by need to avenge the loss of booze—driven by need to be cruel—driven by combat impulses I couldn't imagine—the sergeant muttered, "Redskin huh? Let's see the color of your blood," missing grabbing my arm as I whirled to escape.

The guy who'd mistaken the skunk for his childhood's family pussy stuck out one shining boot, muttering childishly, "Tit for tat! You kill my dog, I'll kill your cat," and stumbling, I fell against the cyclone fence, just able to claw myself upright in time to face the huge sergeant, in his upraised hand the broken bottle, its jagged end a butchering blade, bright beneath the gate light.

Did I warn him? "Yes," I could say, the gun in my hand all the warning any sane man would have needed.

The combat veteran had probably not been sane for a long time, and driven by whatever insanity of my own, I disobeyed Dad's command that I never point a gun at a man unless I intended to kill him. Aiming instead at a high-shine, good-time boot, I squeezed—did not pull, Captain—*squeezed* the trigger, as the army had taught. I'd forgotten or did not have time to heed Dad's advice about cocking before shooting. The double-action mechanism jerked the barrel up. My bullet shattered the thighbone, but because it missed the main artery, a man who'd gone unwounded through two wars was lucky again and didn't bleed to death, even though his skunk-loving buddy drowsed and let go of the belt I'd twisted as a tourniquet. My running, "bad" heart furiously pumping, to get help and save my attacker's life, saved me from prison; but I'd shot a hero of not one but two wars and delayed his second triumphal return to a welcoming hometown. "Accidental discharge of weapon" satisfied the army's concerns and added to my and to my warrior forebears' long-ago humiliation, but I'd won some sort of Cherokee victory in the only history that really matters, the one in one's own head. I got off with a reprimand and got out of the army, a possibly rabid fellow mammal and a certainly drunk and probably insane fellow American my only victims, my only war wounds those from immunization shots.

# PART THREE

# All in the Family: Some Vanishing American Military Histories

# A Vanishing American's First Struggles against Vanishing

Natal cord an Indian necktie noosed around Juke's neck, hands tore him free, swatted his butt, and startled into the air, which he and the world had to share, a throat-clearing squall. War cries, words of love, social insights, unanswerable philosophical questions—everything he'd ever be able to utter depended on that first protest, against that first swat.

If he'd vanished into the earth at birth, he'd not have heard men say, "And another redskin bit the dust," meaning they'd emptied another bottle, or meaning they'd dinged, zapped, or wasted—not a man, not a woman, not a child, but an enemy.

Into invaders' folk sayings, folkways, massacres, official histories, and marital or other minglings, Vanishing Americans had been vanishing for approximately five hundred years. Forests had disappeared into house walls and smoke up chimneys. Whole tribes had disappeared into the smoke of cannons, the only memory left of them descendants of enemies' memories. Indian hunting grounds had been cut into half- or quarter-mile-wide farms, the Sacred Earth drawn and quartered, as were bodies of pigs that Juke would help butcher—as were human bodies in history books. The Indian heritage of Juke's father, Dirk Dark Cloud, had been drawn—that of his children, Parm, Ann, and Juke, quartered.

Her first child lost to illness, Juke's German-American mother tended, winter after winter, night after sleepless night, her surviving children, heating turpentine-and-lard-soaked rags over a kerosene lamp and safety-pinning comforting warmth between wool undershirts and phlegm-strictured chests. To quell coughing, Juke's Cherokee-English father steeped flakes shaved off a sassafras root, then laced this New World medicine-tea with the Old World's cure-all or kill-all spirits, which he drank to drive off spirits of enemies he'd killed in World War Two.

"Most of what we live remains a mystery," one of Juke's teachers, old and wise, would say mysteriously. Resurrected in the mind, he could not tell why Juke woke to bullet-shattered glass clattering onto his baby bed. From heaven, Juke's mother could not add to her story of shielding Juke's blanket-swaddled body, although window fragments cut her arms. From the Spirit Land, Juke's father could not name the dark shape escaping, becoming one with the darkness, in which no bullet—fired for revenge or to prevent a future attack—could find its target.

School would tell of civilization bestowed. Juke's European American–Vanishing American family would tell of glass shards falling, and falling snow.

Generations before Juke lived, Iowa pioneers had lynched the last renegade redskin and skinned the last wild bear, but while golden-tressed Ma hugged, rocked, and read to her dark-haired Goldilocks and dark-pelted cubs, Pa's coveralls, hung to dry above the black-barred wood-stove's blazing stockades, seemed to Juke to be Cherokees, dancing on air, below gallows. And Pa's Kentucky boyhood's bear, as black as a thunder cloud, would roar after lambs. Lunging and plunging on all fours, playing at inflicting and at escaping death, Juke's big brother Parm would savor mawfuls of delicious syllables, "GROWL! GROWL! GRR! GRR!" lamp flame reflecting off black-gapped teeth, while Juke and Ann, his sister, would gleefully bleat, "Baa, Baa, Beah, Beah," scrambling and gamboling over tobacco tins tacked flat to cover holes that months back, Pa—drunkenly yelling, "Durned little nigger-skinned Indniun"—had shot around Juke's feet.

His quite pale English-Cherokee father's darkest-skinned child, Juke heard "Durned little nigger-skinned Indniun" whenever his father got crazy drunk. Grown to manhood, Juke would tell friends that he'd survived an in-the-family Indian War, continuing generations after his outgunned Cherokee forebears had fled to wooded hills and into that flimsy sanctuary, memory. The second in-the-family war Juke survived was World War Two, supposedly won years before Juke's entering the world, but fought again and again when memories, buried like land mines, exploded in Juke's usually loving father's alcohol-addled mind, causing him to shoot wildly at the ghosts of men he'd actually killed.

"'Doughboys,' they called our fathers when they got sent to fight, and doughboys was what they shoulda called us GI's in World War Two, because we was just like our fathers, killing and dying to keep the rich rolling in dough," Pa told play-soldiers Parm and Juke.

Sun glittering off eagle-emblem buttons, Juke's grandpa, his Pa's doughboy daddy, had marched—in puttees wound like bandages around legs, in choke-collared uniform coat and in go-to-hell cap—through a victory blizzard of Wall Street ticker tape, while orators had orated that Americans were Manifestly Destined to plunder others forever—none of the wealthy speakers guessing that confetti-ticker-tape's numbers would add up to—and subtract to—the 1929 depression.

"I'd growed up hungry, and—a moldy bread crust or whatever—I always gived half of what I had," Pa said, recalling that children's small, chilblained fingers had tugged at the trench coat he still wore as a farmer's chore coat. "Little kids," he told his own little kids, and he said, "Only little Finland was honest enough to pay its war debt after World War One, but—never learn, never learn—them big-shot rich fellers got us mixed up in World War Two, and then in Korea, and just in time for you, Parm, and you, Juke, they'll get us into another ruckus, as sure as God made little Green Apples."

"The War to End All Wars," propagandists had named Pa's Pa's war, and "the Four Freedoms War" was what they'd named Pa's. At play, some days, sister Ann would decide, "You be soldiers again"—sticks for guns, pans for helmets, repair-rivets in one as shiny as bullets—"and I'll be your nurse"—scissoring bandages from newspapers whose headlines included a word short enough to be easily read, even by a little child, WAR!

Yanking his cardboard trench knife from between Nurse Ann's ribs and red-crayon-cross-banded arm, big brother Parm, the Nazi, would aim a black stick, and—BANG! you're dead!

Fallen onto a soft, brown pile of last fall's fallen, little brother Juke would peek, between supposedly closed-forever lids, at crimson leaves, spinning, like Pa's stories' flaming warplanes, down, and would not rise until he was commanded to be, again, alive. Because she was something called a Republican, Ma said, "I like Ike because he makes us safe. He beat those Nazis, and he'll beat these communists and make us safe. I like Ike."

Sticking straight up at heaven what was left of a finger he used to use to play banjo for a lot of people, not just for his wife and kids, Pa muttered, "There's the goddamned war you say your big-shot general won."

Because Pa was something that he called an Indniun, he said words that Christians could not say or God would wash out their mouths with soap. Because Pa was something Ma called a Democrat, he told Ma, "It's me and men like me that's going to keep the country safe, not that damned bastard general."

The damned general was a bastard, but that didn't mean that the damned general's daddy hadn't married the damned general's mommy. The damned general was a bastard because he took food out of working people's mouths and his rich friends got fat.

Big brother Parm had stopped crying and was snoring beside Juke, but Juke's hungry feelings were little chickens pecking to get out of eggs, and Juke was afraid he'd be like his sister, with a hole in his belly for peepee, or be, like the baby brother born before Juke was born, buried under a little stone.

After a meal with no meat except the taste of it in lard on bread, Juke would climb onto a chair, blow to melt eyeholes in frost, and watch for Pa.

Smoke signals rising from a scarf he'd tied like a Wild West bandit mask over his nose, hands shoved into pockets, bang-bang black-barreled shotgun wedged into army-surplus-overcoated armpit, Pa would finally come slogging through thigh-deep snowdrifts, burlap game bag blowing back from shoulder strap, empty—or bouncing as if alive, weighted by dead pheasant or dead rabbit.

The calendar's winter was over, but not the thermometer's.

No vegetable-crammed jars gleaming on pantry shelves, potato pile in rat-smell cellar dwindling, and only soup bones left of the pig hung to freeze in the woodshed, Ann, Parm, and Juke were taking their minds off hunger by chasing each other on all fours and gleefully butting—like Booey-Head Bull Calves, doomed to the butcher's blade.

Parm and Ann were enjoying making Juke feel big—or enjoying making themselves feel little again, by letting Juke scare them—but all three kids were scared when they heard Pa yelling, "Banks makes a man feel damned small. My word ain't good enough. They got to have this goddamned paper a man can't understand except where to sign it. I'll work, work, work and starve till I drop, and there's nothing I can do about it—NOTHING—not a goddamned thing—NOTHING!"

Ma sincerely hoped that Pa had not made things *worse* by using profanity in the presence of a lady—a lady who counted money inside a brass-barred cage in the bank, and talked to everyone in town, including the priest.

Pa made things *better*—for himself—by belting down corn whiskey, homemade from home-grown corn—White Lightning. Bolt after bolt struck the brain of a man humiliated one goddamned time too many, and he was again up on what Ma called his high horse. He was Saul proclaiming his sin of pride in being a man, by God, a man, and a goddamned good one, not no worse than nobody else! He was miraculously *delivered* from the goddamned banker. He was *delivered* from kids' bellyaching about empty bellies; and he was *delivered* from a lady who thinks she's too good for an Indniun husband!

As White Lightning thundered from a mouth that had, last night, sung lullabies, Juke's sister and brother grabbed coats and ran to hide among calves in the warm barn. No longer a fierce Booey-Head Bull Calf, but a small, terrified child—a Child of God, according to Ma's priest—Juke hid under the table and heard, despite grimy hands clamped over unwashed ears, an Indian Adam accuse his stolen rib's Christian people of stealing land, after murdering Indians.

Peeking between table leg and chair legs, Juke saw Ma miss grabbing Pa's pistol.

Juke had seen, through a cloud risen from his own cold nose, that pistol explode smoke into chilling air, and seen breath shoot out of a big pig's bloody snout, then stop.

After being hung from a hook, hammered behind yellow teeth, and plunged into a barrelful of scalding water, the pig had been scraped till its skin was as smooth as Juke's own, then split, guts uncoiling—pale snakes dangling from the jaws of the family dog and slithering away through snow, leaving twisty red trails between pawprints.

Pa's shadow threatening Ma's shadow on the wall, Juke heard that it was the damned Republicans fault there was only lard-flavored bread left to eat.

Ma said it was Pa's darned Democrats who'd got him wounded in the goshdarned war and got her first husband killed, and Juke's sinfully unwashed ears heard what German forebears had heard, a moment of their lives, a moment of their nation's history, marked by the chiming of the family clock—the clock brought by Juke's mother's mother's mother to America and not to be sold, not for any amount of money, not even if everyone starved to death.

One of those who'd starve to keep time chiming—a Child of God—Juke promised his Heavenly Father he'd scrub his ears, even though wash-bucket water was as cold as ice melting off kindling he'd carried to the stove, and he would not ever again squabble with his sister and brother, if only Ma would not bleed like the pig and be dead.

Over the bawling of the calves they hid among—the calves whose only hope was all of Earth's creatures' hope, to be warm and fed until becoming food themselves—Juke's brother and sister heard the Armageddon thunder of Pa's gun. Bullet-damaged clock chiming, chiming, more hours of lives than there were for all day, Juke heard Ma scream, "Why not kill me, instead? And kill the children, too. That's what you want, isn't it—isn't it? Then you'd be on the road again, playing your banjo and singing and—and kissing loose women again. Then you'd be free!"

Scrambling up onto trembling legs, Juke lowered his head and charged—charged big, bayonet-scarred fists—charged big-pig-killing gun—Juke's Booey-Head Bull Calf bellows, of anguish, of rage, as berserk as the clock's dying chimes.

Pa helpless, flabbergasted by fury his sperm had become, Ma had to defend him against her defender. With one arm, she caught and held her child's sobbing skull's small accumulation of sorrows and joys, and with the other arm hugged her sobbing husband's years-greater accumulation.

Juke would be awarded two medals for killing strangers, but his first warrior deed was not commemorated by any eagle-embossed army document.

"Juke Dark Cloud, you durned little wild Indniun, your mother and me it must of been it was we was having some spat like husband and wife sometimes they will, but you—you had you more grit than I'd knowed you'd had," was Pa's way of remembering a moment when generations before and generations beyond Juke's life had been the slight squeeze of a trigger finger from obliteration—a moment when Juke's and all people's eventual end was foretold by the death-knell tolling of the family clock.

# Laugh before Breakfast

"Laugh before breakfast, and you'll cry before supper," Parm Dark Cloud's mother told him, her bruised cheek all there was to be seen of Parm's dad.

His dad was what eight-year-old Parm knew of World War Two—his dad winning it again when telling his admiring children stories of combat, and losing it when he'd spend a once-a-month disability check to get insanely, violently drunk in Custer's Bottomless Keg, the bar whose topless waitresses would serve Indians. When drinking, veterans fought, again, America's wars—with words, with fists, and sometimes with knives or with guns. Veterans of machine-age war fought the Indian Wars, citing treaties as if they'd read them, or proclaiming Manifest Destiny as inevitable as a weather system moving from ocean inland. Veterans fought the Civil War, in which great-great-grandfathers had tried, with musket mini-balls and cannonballs, to kill one another, and had, to a horrifying extent, succeeded. Young again, grandfathers fought again the War to End All Wars, a war without end in memories—of bayonets and poison gas, of eating some French farmer's mud-and-manure-stained beets while sitting on the stacked corpses of Huns. Young again, amid shimmering drinks and the comforting breasts of waitresses, middle-aged fathers fought again the war that had amputated one of Parm's father's banjo-chording fingers, some toes, and part of his mind.

Last night, Parm's dad had been remembering Italian women, while hardworking American waitresses' tip-soliciting laughter had jiggled glistening sweat off lipsticked nipples.

Parm's mom had been in the living room, listening to men and women singing on the blank TV that still had sound, and watching dark lips move over gleaming teeth on a mute second TV that still had its picture.

Their mom preoccupied with television's finger-sized women and men's jollity and frivolity, and with brooding over their dad's naughtiness, Parm and his brother Juke stayed up late, blocking mouse holes with shoes, then chasing mice around and around their room and suffering tiny bites and letting their squirming prey escape. The mouse hunt kept Parm from worrying that his dad might come home and shoot wildly, again—and from worrying that his dad might not come home, ever, as had happened with other fathers when jobs were lost and unemployment money ran out and there were too many mouths and too many months till next spring's gardens—and fewer and fewer deer to poach off thinly forested hills.

"Laugh before breakfast—cry before supper."

At dawn, Parm's brother Juke, five, and their sister Ann, six, had come tumbling onto Parm's cot, and they'd all three started tickling each other's scrawny ribs, forgetting that their giggling might wake their dad, who had stumbled home and hit their mom while she'd been trying to persuade him to get some sleep.

The little kids' tickling fingers making him feel little again, Parm's dread of a long day in a crowded school, his fear of white kids' bullying, and even his fear of his drunken father's bullets disappeared into laughter. Most mornings when the little kids squirmed onto his cot, Parm would wake up happy; but some mornings he'd wake up grouchy and pull on clothes and escape into the outdoor toilet, called "the backhouse."

Parm liked to linger in the one place where he could be by himself. After wiping with order forms from last year's mail-order catalog, he'd turn page after glossy page, imagining that toy army tanks and planes and real hunting rifles and knives were his. Bashful, he'd only glance at the pages of women, bare except for underwear brighter than any that hung on neighboring families' laundry lines. The pestering little kids had once pursued their big brother into the backhouse, and their mother had whipped her children's legs, using her husband's broad, flat razor strop, whipping Parm along with the little ones.

Decreeing that only one person should be in the backhouse at one time, even though there were two holes, Parm's mother's voice had sounded as it had when her kids had played among cemetery stones, their war whoops louder than the priest's funeral ritual. From the sense of taboo in his white, Christian mother's voice, and from his Indian father's choosing to pee and take dumps behind bushes, Parm knew there was something bad about the backhouse. Windowless, it was gloomy, even in brightest sunlight, and lurking in its black depths was something worse than anything that had ever passed from his body and back into the earth.

The little kid he had been and the man he was going to be simultaneously alive as his tingling fingers turned catalog pages, Parm always lingered longer than he had to in the backhouse, even though it was scarier than the hayloft, where hoboes might lurk like storybook trolls—scarier than the cellar, where rats scurried among shadows while you filled a pail with potatoes. Scarier than the backhouse was the world in Parm's drunken father's voice, his army voice, his killer voice, as terrible as his bullets, which had, two or three months back, splintered white wood out of gray floor around Parm's brother Juke's little feet.

Mornings when their dad slept, still stunned by drinks that had released the happiness of youth, and then the horrors of war, the children's giggles would bring their mother running. Her face as terrified as it had been the time she'd found Parm climbing the windmill's seventy feet of exciting danger, she'd clamp the first mouth in reach, then a second mouth, if it hadn't stopped its giggling in time. If she'd only whispered, "Dad," the kids would have shut up as if grabbed, because they didn't want him to awake either; but they were eight, five, and two, and they couldn't remember—until their mother's hand, which had lovingly tended them so long, clamped and hurt their lips against their own teeth. "My God, what are you boys trying to do?" she'd say—"*boys*," though she'd grab their sister's giggling mouth, too.

When sober, Parm's daddy would sing English ballads, Americanized in the Appalachian Mountains, where he had grown up. His dream of becoming a Grand Old Opry performer had ended when shrapnel slashed one finger from his banjo-chording hand. He'd still been able to make a living as a traveling musician, but then he'd played for a dance in Custer, South Dakota, and met a war widow who'd inherited a few acres of corn, oats, hay, and pasture—a few pigs, a few cows, and a dozen or so chickens. The buildings included a barn, a hog house, a chicken house, a backhouse, and a farmhouse, one with electricity but without indoor plumbing.

Most nights, after hard farm work was done, and before he drove off to eight more hours of work as a factory janitor, Parm's Good Dad, his Sober Dad, would hold Parm's sister and brother on his war-wound-weakened knee, and hold Parm on the stronger. TV's news of new war turned down low in the living room, Parm dad would tell his little ones some of his glory moments, in battles fought reassuringly long ago. His story-telling voice like his soothing, lullaby-singing voice, he'd tell about killing "some of them highfalutin fellers what does the planning, them enemy offysirs."

Once, his telescopic sight had found a white-haired man so important, the enemy soldiers had not only saluted but had bowed.

"That old colonel or general, he looked," Parm's daddy mused, "like the gentleman you are named for—Parmenter, my old great uncle what always gave me candy when he'd see me, after my daddy he passed on.

"The old enemy offysir I'm talking about, he was wearing one of those white too-nicks, they calls them, and in the middle of a lot of blue and purple ribbons on his chest, he had him a red ribbon, with a gold cross hung from it. They was other offysirs, too, all wearing clean clothes and high boots, which some poor boy of their army had probably had to shine that morning—ten offysirs, counting the old one, and I didn't have but the nine dum-dums, those bullets I'd cut the tips off of, so's they'd flatten when they struck and tear a lot of meat. Nine bullets, you understand, just like the fingers on my hands, minus the one." He crooked what was left of the wounded one down. "Or toes." He looked at Parm's brother Juke's bare toes and paused, as if counting, as if maybe trying to remember if he hadn't shot one off the last time he was drunk, his pistol bullets tearing wood floor as his rifle bullets had torn enemies' flesh.

Parm's brother's toes were quivering like baby mice, afraid when a pitchfork lifted the hay that had roofed their nest, but it was Parm's sister's littlest toe that her daddy finally reached out and bent down. Parm's sister giggled and went on with the girl story she always mumbled to herself during her daddy's war-time/sleepy-time stories.

Now, Parm was happy, too, reassured that this was his Good Dad, clasping his children to his bony chest as if they were parts of his own body he was afraid might fall off—like maybe they were pieces of the rib that got took out of Adam in the story Parm's teacher had tried to read before everybody started giggling and goosing each other in the sides. She'd slammed her big black book shut and called all the children Heathen Indians, though most were blond.

"There was," Parm's father was continuing, "one young man what could of been the old commander offysir's son from the look of the thin nose. I gived the young one a patch of red on his chest that made the old offysir's crimson medal ribbon look like a dribble running out a nose after a fist fight.

"The next target I took just under the rim of one of them dishpan-shape helmets they thought they was so safe wearing. I knowed it was a important offysir I was getting because there was little gold curlycues on his blue collar.

"Them offysirs they was all panicky by this time, except for the old man. He just stood there, looking down at the young feller I'd kilt the first. The others, the rest of them still alive, they was running and falling this way and that way like they was doing a dance for the benefit of the ordinary soldiers, what had been made to salute and so on. Them offysirs was dancing, and every drum beat from yours truly's gun, another offysir would fall and scrabble around all bloody on the ground, until them fine uniforms was more messed up than my own mud-daubed cammyflodge clothes. The ordinary soldiers they was down on their bellies, shooting at wind-stirring leaves and wondering who'd be next in my sights. They needn't of worried. There wasn't but one bullet left in my gun. I had my extry loaded clip, sure, but I'd need that if some enemy soldiers cut me off before I could shinny down from my tree and get myself back behind our own side's lines.

"During all my shooting, the old baron or field marshal or earl or whatever he was, he just stood there erect, like he was in front of a battalion on parade all for his bennyfit, and not in front of his whole rettynew of dead offysirs and the ordinary soldiers twisting around like big fishworms trying to tunnel deeper into the mud. The old gentleman, he had these black leather gloves clasped together up to his white-uniformed, gold-flower-stitched chest right under all them rainbow ribbons and the red ribbon like a trickle of blood above the gold cross. He was doing him some praying, that old boy was, right over the body of what was probably all that was left of his own fine son, and the old offysir father's white chest it was moving up and down with words which was probably half sobbing by then, and that big gold cross was quivering and quavering and glittering and sparking, like God himself was answering.

"I let the old gentleman go."

"You let him go? Aw, Daddy, you didn't let him go-o." Parm thought his father was teasing, like he sometimes did, and might answer, "I let him go, just like you boys lets the mousey-mousey go, for the fun of catching him again." Instead, he said, "Yes, if that old gentleman had got a medal that good and everybody liked him so good they'd bend the knee to him, he was just too good to kill. Besides, he had him a beard the shape of a Indniun spear point, just like Great Uncle Parm's beard, except white, not black, and he looked like Great Uncle Parm might of looked if he'd lived to get old instead of kicking the bucket account of having breathed the same poison gas what had took my dad.

"They was nine offysirs in that rettynew of high mucky-muck Eye-tal-yuns. Eight I'd already got, and I had one dum-dum left in my gun. The number nine offysir, he'd flopped down in the mud, trying to hide amongst the bodies of the others he'd sat at breakfast with just minutes ago, more'n likely; but even though I'd been shooting fast, my mind had been taking everything in, the whole while, and I put my crosshair sights right on the seam between the neat stitched hip pockets up in the air, still clean amongst all them others what had wiggled around and got themselves all messy like hogs in a hog wallow, and I gived that high mucky-muck last guy a new cornhole the biggest bear in our woods could of relieved itself out of without suffering no discomfort.

"And, yeah, I just left the old duke or prince or whatever standing there, all erect and fine looking in front of his soldiers, who didn't give a tinker's damn by now if it was a angel itself standing all shiny and clean and wondrous looking in front of them. He was lucky he was the spitting image of Uncle Parmenter, so rich and well-dressed and proud and so good to me when I was little. Only maybe he wasn't lucky, if it was his son I'd plinked number one, and the old man left sad and forlorn and praying for one more bullet to send him after his boy.

"'Why didn't you kill that old colonel or general?' our own high mucky-mucks askt.

"'Because he was a better man than any of you,' I felt like telling them, but in the army, a lots of the time you got to lie. It's like putting grass in a net on your helmet to keep from getting shot. "'The nine I killed was standing around the old white-haired gentleman, hiding him from my sights,' I said. 'They was very brave offysirs, right out there with the men.'

"'They were enemies,' a bald old major told me. He knew danged well I had in mind him and his own rettynew awearing warm, clean uniforms and sitting around their stove and keeping me standing, like some school kid, answering questions. Wore-out and wet and muddy and cold from two days and nights with just my thin cammyflodge coat to cover me, I wanted to up with my rifle and give the major some red to trickle down amongst them rainbow battle ribbons he probably hadn't ever had to stir from his little canvas stool to get given to him; but I answered, 'They are Good Enemies, Sir—Dead Enemies, Sir,' and remembering the saying 'The only Good Indniun is a Dead Indniun,' all of them offysirs laughed, pleased that their Indniun sniper had killed them some enemies and was joking about it."

Parm's brother and sister were laying their little tousley heads against their dad's chest, which was now scarcely moving with the softening, slowing voice—Parm's dad sounding as sleepy as his children, though he'd soon go off to his janitor job, to get money for food and, sometimes, to go and get crazy drunk.

"Laugh before breakfast."

Flag-flaunting caskets had celebrated victory in two world wars.

"Cry before supper."

Earth-colored body bags would be flown home from defeat in Parm's war, the war in Vietnam.

Like America itself, Parm had two fathers—one loving, one not—and hearing, "Laugh before breakfast, and you'll cry before supper," Parm's fear was worse because for a time, he'd felt that his father and the whole world—with its two sun-warmed hemispheres, and God's great star-sparkly sky around them—was good.

# The Chicken Affliction and a Man of God

"Today," Juke Dark Cloud's mother hopefully stated, "is the beginning of the rest of my life." She paused, to give herself and her children time to believe something that had, somehow, sounded better when she'd heard it on TV. "Today, when Dirk Dark Cloud comes home, cussing and screaming and shooting at Germans as dead as doornails already and not attacking anybody for years, why, yes, today, yes, Dirk Dark Cloud is going to come up against a Force a whole lot stronger than Hitler and all those other dead Nazis put together."

"This Force, it's Father O'Mara, isn't it?" Juke asked, and when his mother emphatically nodded, sun flashing pale lightning from white hairs among the dark, he reminded her, "We usually only go to church when there's a wedding or a funeral."

"In church and out, I've prayed and prayed to God," Juke's mother told her two sons and her only daughter, her words ones she had always sobbed, to comfort them, whenever their father had come home drunk and abusive. "This time—just like the Air Force bombers providing air support for invasions and so on—this time, there'll be help from On High. When Father O'Mara sees our truck come up this hill, he will drive down from our neighbors. Father O'Mara has converted more than a few, and he will convert Dirk Dark Cloud from a once-a-month drunk Indian to a once-a-week Christian Indian."

Sunday dinner was chicken—not with the fat-yellowed fluffy dumplings Juke and his brother Parm and his sister Ann liked, but with the hard Cherokee kind their father liked—and the distant courthouse clock had just chimed noon when, as punctual as tomorrow's school bus's flashing lights would be, sun threw windshield glitters up from where the clay farm road joined gleaming blacktop highway. Hidden among pines as it climbed, Dirk Dark Cloud's truck raised dust, leaving a ghost-gray road hovering in breezeless air.

Though almost ten—able to remember last night's fear and dread, and able to remember last month's bullets' splintering floor around his muddy shoes—Juke was, like people older than himself, not quite able to believe what he very well knew, and instead of going into hiding before his drunken father's arrival, he waited on the porch—waited, like centuries of other children, for the Kingdom of the Child to triumph over the bullying tantrums of grown men.

As if in answer to Juke's mother's prayers, her priest's car's powerful engine made itself heard, its echoing off the neighbors' farm buildings, half a mile uphill, sounding and resounding like a World-War-Two-movie bomber squadron, and at that moment, around a final curve, the Dark Cloud family's transportation appeared. Mud, dust, and rust were its paint, but bare steel gleamed silver from fenders that had been scraped anew against canyon walls. What had saved Dirk Dark Cloud when there was only air between him and a drop of hundreds of feet might have been the luck of drunkards, or it might have been the deity Juke's mother believed would save everyone.

The rusty truck bouncing off the red-white-and blue U.S. mailbox's rusty steel post, then off a wooden gatepost and into the narrow lane, Juke's father—confusing accelerator with brake, or taking jealous revenge—sped over flowers planted in red-and-white flag-stripe flower-garden rows, to honor Juke's mother's dead, and forever young, war-hero first husband.

Juke, having hopefully waited instead of fearfully hiding, saw that what sounded like his father shooting again some German he'd already killed innumerable times was really the fender-frayed right front tire's bumping against the chicken coop and committing hara-kiri against a nail.

Adapted to waddling from nest to feed pan—to provide breakfast eggs and, eventually, a last supper—chickens thought the tire blowout a rifle shot, like that with which Juke's brother Parm had, this Sunday, already doomed one stewing hen to lie in state in the company of dumplings. Resurrecting ancestral skills, the surviving chickens flew, one after the other, from their radically askew coop's only window, then landed where weak wings and gravity ordained that they land, inside Dirk Dark Cloud's pickup truck's small cab.

From under a slowly growing accumulation of smothering feathers, Juke's father hurled his wife's and most of their community's God's damnation against his chicken affliction, meanwhile helping the Lord to help him by tossing each white-feathered hitchhiker out—past, more often than not, two or three others flying in.

Hearing Juke's father taking the name of God in vain, Juke's mother, her faith in Father O'Mara wavering, cried, "Don't—" doubtless intending to finish with, "let him see you"—meaning Juke—meaning, "Don't let your dark eyes and skin remind your crazy drunk dad of his own half-breed generation's hunger and cold."

"Don't let him see you." It had taken hold of Juke's way of thinking and caused him to slink around corners even when his dad wasn't drunk. His complexion telling the world that he was one of his schoolbook's "Vanishing Americans," Juke wished that he could really, all the way, vanish—like the Greek warrior his teacher had read about, a warrior become invisible so that he could slay a monster.

"Slay." Juke went around chanting the word, the magic sound transcending the bloodying of pheasant, rabbit, or deer—transcending the bloodying of soldiers on the TV News, "SlaySlaySlaySlaySlaySlay" easing fear of what bullets, fired in drunken delirium, might do to a small boy.

"Don't let him—" Juke's mother had started to repeat her warning, but Juke's Sunday-scrubbed face's hopefulness changed "see you" to silence, a silence like that between a congregation's praying and an organist's playing, and Juke stayed put to witness Salvation, a big black Lincoln sedan, entering the gate, one front fender reflecting—its curving transforming to rainbow—the red-white-and-blue U.S. mailbox post. As long as the president's limousine in school magazines, from chrome-toothed, clown-grin grille to brake-light-crimsoned rear bumper, the priest's car stopped, immaculate paint mirroring the dents and scrapes of Dirk Dark Cloud's pickup truck, sun off recently polished silver hubcap bestowing a celestial shimmering on hara-kiri-flat-tire's urine-scribbled, or -dribbled, messages of canines' mating intentions.

The chicken affliction had been temporarily exorcized by Father O'Mara's church vehicle's arrival, but then more wings came flapping hysterically out of the lopsided coop, and Juke's father resumed hurling hens, this time not back the way they had come, but out the driver's-side window and, by accident or by intent, into the priest's car's passenger-side window.

Now it was Father O'Mara's turn to cast out chickens, which Juke's drunken Dad was cursing as Raven Mockers, the Cherokee witch-birds of his nightmares.

Impatient for his white wife's Cherokee dumplings, which had, he knew, been waiting for him all through the battles he had won, or lost, again last night, Juke's father sent what he hoped would be a last, fat stewing hen tumbling, ass over appetite, onto chicken-poop-polka-dotted earth—and, his chicken affliction seemingly finally abated, he got to hell out of the cramped torture oven his truck had become. His exodus gouged his much-dented driver's-side door into Father O'Mara's passenger-side door, and the sound of muddy steel's assault on paint as black as a novice nun's new habit made the old priest go rigid—with only one shoe, as shiny as his parish car, touching ground, but not yet bearing weight.

Seizing her first opportunity, Juke's mother cried, into ominous silence, "Good day, Father. So good of you to stop by," steadfastly carrying out her plan for helping Juke's father to give up alcoholic spirits and to give in to the Spirit of Christianity.

Father O'Mara jostled past his sister in Christ's cordially extended hand and strode straight up to Juke's powerfully built and weakly wobbling father, the old priest's thin arm raised so high his white-haired wrist thrust inches out of its white shirt cuff.

Dirk Dark Cloud drunkenly fumbled in the pocket that usually hid his gun, and Juke's mother's fear took her past the moment when the priest's long life of devoted service, to both whites and Indians, to both Catholics and Protestants, would end in a chicken yard. The servant of the Son of God forgotten, it was to Juke that she cried, "Don't let him see you!"

The Dark Clouds' farm was only a few scrubby acres on an upper slope of Rattlesnake Hill, and sumac bushes were not only adequate cover for the snake that had given the hill its name but also for chicken-thieving coyotes, who always knew enough to get a head start on Juke's father's gunfire. Juke knew he should be obeying his mother's warning and following the coyotes' example, but he was still hoping to see Father O'Mara convert his father from a once-a-month drunken Indian to a once-a-week Christian Indian.

It was not Juke's father's dreaded pistol, it was his dreaded bottle that came out of his suit-coat pocket, and he uncorked it with a meticulousness that reminded Juke of Father O'Mara's movements during weddings or funerals. "Here's mud in your eye, Father," Juke's father mumbled as he took a long drink and nearly lurched past the priest while offering to share.

Skinny arm wobbling as if he had already taken too many drinks, Father O'Mara's pale hand slowly closed around the gold liquid of the nearly full bottle. Juke's father did not let go until Father O'Mara's skeletal fingers had got a good grip.

"Here's mud in *your* eye, you heathen sinner. Ashes to ashes and dust to dust," the old priest intoned. His gaunt wrist rotated; and whiskey, the color of pee, trickling down between gleaming shoes, he moved, with the stately grace of his old, gas-guzzling, parish car, to an ex-oil-barrel trash burner.

Booze, which might have become the glory of today's prolongation of last night's binge, turned earth to mud, as would the not-yet-begun rain, and the shuffling of feet told Juke that his father knew he should be moving, even as Juke's mother's warning had told Juke that he should get out of sight. Knowing was not doing. Alcohol already in Juke's father's brain kept him from saving the alcohol remaining in the bottle. He had not yet taken one step when the gold of draining liquid and the silver of nearly empty glass disappeared beneath the rusty trash-burner rim.

Belatedly, Dirk Dark Cloud lurched into motion, his fingers convulsing, perhaps to try to hold that which was already beyond the reach of any mere mortal hand—perhaps to seize Father O'Mara's scrawny neck and twist it like the neck of a chicken.

Juke's father was still far from realizing his intent when alcohol fumes reached trash-fire embers, and Father O'Mara's white head— bowed as if to pray, but doubtless, really, to confirm the destruction of evil—vanished into a blazing nimbus.

From it, he emerged—white hair, combed forward over a receding hairline, now scorched black, although blue eyes were blinking, unharmed, beneath eyebrows still as white as little arcs of springtime's last snow, surviving in shady hollows up on Rattlesnake Hill.

As Juke backed across the creaking porch to get his trembling flesh out of sight, sounds of his Vanishing American son's attempt to vanish reached Dirk Dark Cloud's drunken brain. Remembering the loss of his bottle, he inched his bayonet-scarred hand into his blue suit-coat pocket, taking time to get a good grip on his pistol.

Juke was several feet from the house corner when his father's carefully oiled blue-black gun barrel began reflecting the trash barrel's resurrected blaze and impending lightning's flickering.

Juke was almost ten, and for years he'd known that he was the gun's target, but Father O'Mara must have figured, logically, that the weapon was intended for him.

That thought should have sent him scurrying into his big black car, but Father O'Mara was a splendid man, who had been an army chaplain in the same war with Juke's father, and Father O'Mara had come to perform a duty.

At the sight of the pistol he'd been summoned to prevent from harming anyone, all of the priest's righteous anger returned, and his impassioned stride, right up to the muzzle of the gun, was such an image of hope that Juke delayed still longer his escape.

"Don't you dare raise your hand to God's man, you—you sybarite. Give me that," Father O'Mara commanded, his old voice faint like the distant thunder but powerful like the thunderstorm really was—and his "that" turned the deadly .45-caliber automatic army-surplus pistol into something contemptible.

Juke thought of the picture of God as a strong old man, and hope became belief—the belief that his father would obey Father O'Mara and give up the pistol and feel better, as Juke always did when he'd obeyed his usually sober dad and his always sober mother and stopped his mischief.

If Father O'Mara had just followed through on what he was saying, if he'd grabbed the pistol, which he had said must be given to him, maybe Juke's father's fingers, faithful to a brain trained to obey commands, would have given up the gun, and maybe a different life for the Dark Cloud family could have begun, as Juke's mother had dared to hope.

But like his Savior, Father O'Mara was part divine and part merely man. The actual meaning of his command had meant no more to him than his loudly shouted "Sybarite" had meant to a nine-year-old schoolboy. Instead of seizing the pistol, the fierce-tempered old bachelor slapped the uncomprehending Indian face, as he'd reportedly slapped that of many a defiant reservation-orphanage child, and when pale, fragile fingers rebounded off hard, black-whiskered jaw, a gunshot sounded, and echoed and echoed.

Juke had last seen the blue-black muzzle pointed at the priest's red-veined nose, but dust spurted up between shiny shoes, and spurted again and again as the old man skipped backward.

Not giving Father O'Mara a chance to regain courage, Juke's father kept on firing until the priest, who had fled face toward the pistol, as if to keep its bullets from striking him, backed into the driver's seat of his car. The starter whirred, the powerful engine caught, and with a roar that obliterated still-distant thunder, the old car surged forward, its gleaming fender sideswiping the askew chicken coop, sending chickens into a flight that ended with their flapping down short of the gleaming rear bumper and the ghost-gray exhaust.

Juke knew there was one bullet left in his father's gun—he had counted for too many years not to know—and it occurred to him, in superstitious dread, that he was nine years old, not quite ten. He knew he ought to have been around the corner of the house a long time ago, but now his mother's "Don't let him see you" meant "Don't attract attention by moving," and obediently standing still, Juke saw Father O'Mara's old face throw back an enraged and terrified last glance, blue eyes intense blue pieces of sky under bangs charred storm-cloud black.

Slowly, Juke's father's gun rose, and Juke could imagine the black car careening, shattered glass's shards a halo of silver thorns around the Man of God's head, the pale old face twisting down, all bloody, to hang by its frail chin from jagged window glass.

Body still turned as if tracking the escaping priest, Dirk Dark Cloud twisted his head around, and then his arm, and shot a chicken off the roof of his pickup, mumbling, "Sunday, by God! I want my dumplings."

Its white breast spurting red, the bird spread its generations-shortened wings to try to escape the death that had already overtaken it. A plump paraclete, it jolted up into a stiff-winged, awkward cross, and then it fell, onto the chicken-poop-polka-dotted chicken yard.

Not yet ten, and not ready to accept his mortal destiny, Juke, a Vanishing American, ran, hoping to vanish temporarily and escape permanently vanishing.

He heard cartridges clicking into clip, heard one's being wrenched into the firing chamber.

The first bullet made dust spurt just ahead of him, and the second bullet hit the trunk of a bush he'd just reached. Over the sound of his pounding feet, he heard a rattlesnake's warning and slowed and veered. Just in time, he sidestepped some crumpled news his father had used for toilet-paper and ran to the next bush, fifty feet uphill. He heard his mother yell something about "Sheriff," and he heard his father yell one of the words he'd always forbidden his kids to say.

Juke saw white wood flare out of black bark, heard the shot, and in two leaps he was behind the bush and there was another just beyond and another, and then hail struck like silver bullets, screening him from his father's bullets, and he ran and ran up the hill until he was over the top, where he hid, hungry and wet and shivering among boulders.

He'd learn, from his sister and brother, that the second coming of Father O'Mara had caught their slowly sobering father in the middle of his second helping of chicken and Cherokee dumplings, a meal that a forgiving priest and a hungry law-enforcement officer were glad to share, before the latter delivered his usual sermon on excessive drinking and the reckless discharge of a firearm.

While the Old World devoted itself to rebuilding bombed homes, factories, and cathedrals, on New World TV, Juke's mother lived another day of her life, ministering to her war-damaged husband and to her war-damaged children and praying that there would never be another war.

# Hole Soldiers, Madonna and Child

Flamethrowers moving away from the tunnel's two charred entrances, the captain nicknamed Captain Alabama shouted, "You there, Parm Dark Cloud—Spick, Indniun, Dago, whatever you are—I need me somebody small, from one of them underfed and undervitamined races. I need me a Hole Soldier."

White soldiers thought their captain's joking racism was funny, but I didn't laugh, and neither did the captain's other Hole Soldier, a scrawny sixteen-year-old black kid, who'd pretended to be eighteen in order to enlist and get out of whatever he had to get out of back home.

My face and hands daubed black for my crawl into darkness, the captain pretended to be mystified. "Which one is you?"

"Sir, I'm damned if I know," I answered.

"Order number one," the captain told the black kid and me, "don't shoot each other. Order number two, shoot anybody else."

I'd been scared to start with, and I was more scared after a long wait with nothing to do but swat insects deviling the back of my neck. After awhile there wasn't any more smoke—from charred roots inside the tunnel or from supplies or from bodies. Following the captain's orders,

I wrapped a machine pistol's sling around my forearm so it couldn't be wrenched out of my grip, slid a long flashlight into my left jacket sleeve, and pressed my eyes into my right forearm to accustom myself to darkness. "In you go! Move! Move!" Captain Alabama commanded, gouging his rifle against my ribs, even though I'd already gotten down onto my belly and had started to crawl.

The captain knew what he was doing. As soon as my shoulders blocked off the last daylight, I couldn't make myself crawl further until I felt boot edges either side of my thighs and knew that if I tried to back out, I'd be looking into a rifle muzzle. I don't think I believed the captain would shoot me. Probably, if I'd been able to think about it, I'd have guessed he'd have cuffed me around to get me out of my panic, and then have stuffed my head back into the tunnel. Whatever I thought or didn't, those hard boot edges got me going again.

The searing heat of flamethrowers had been absorbed, and only rocks were still warm to the backs of my hands sliding past, right forefinger tensed on trigger, left thumb on flashlight switch. I wanted to flick that switch, but I knew the light would make me a target.

With the first insect sting on my wrist, I had to fight the urge to let go of both gun and flashlight and try to protect my face.

A sting above one eyebrow brought tears, but blotting them against cloth covering my shoulder, I kept on crawling. I tried to estimate the distance I'd crawled and the extent of darkness I must still crawl through, but I was too scared and disoriented to remember my count.

A snake slithering along the back of my gun hand stopped when, paralyzed by terror, I stopped; and, after a while, I realized it was a root, still moist this far from a flamethrower's reach.

Friction of coveralls now quiet, since I wasn't crawling, I could hear something not far ahead. It stopped. I waited, thumb on flashlight switch, finger on trigger.

The movement started toward me again, louder, nearer than I'd thought. Insects were crawling over my few inches of bare skin, and something was crawling into my jacket collar; but, probably because I was motionless, there were no stings.

Light blinded me, and I'd all but squeezed the trigger before "It's me" sounded, and I yelled back, "It's me!"

When the light shifted, I saw the black kid crawl out of his tunnel and drop into a small pit. In it, a woman was kneeling as if she were at prayer, her eyes closed, black lashes gleaming with tears, which were slow to dry in this damp place. Locked in the woman's arms, a child was looking right at my flashlight but not blinking.

"Goddamn," the black kid said. "I figured they'd be dead after them flamethrowers either'd cooked them or burned up all their oxygen, like these two, but I kept feeling people ahead of me."

When he said it, it seemed so real, I swung my flashlight all around again, and when I did, he did the same; but our intense white lights showed no other tunnels. There had been no escape, and no one else was here, just the staring child and the young mother, a crucifix dangling from her pale palm.

With us on our knees, because of the low ceiling over the shallow pit, it was like kneeling in front of a Madonna and child, even though I was not a Christian and had only been to weddings and funerals in an Indian reservation church.

"Let's get 'em roped together to drag 'em out," the black kid said.

"Let's leave them."

"But it's orders—for body count."

"We could just say there's nobody in here." He said, "I'll say it if you say it."

We said it, and after explosives were detonated, the tunnel, where I'd been terrified in darkness, collapsed, leaving a small depression in the earth.

"Make a damned good latrine ditch, and none of you dogfaces has to sweat to dig it," the captain said and squared away to take a piss.

"I don't think I want to stick around for this," the black kid said. We'd just started to get out of clay-slimed coveralls. Back in the U.S., people could change TV channels. We endured midday heat and itching sweat in insect bites awhile longer, and walked away, not to have to see.

# A Sybarite and One of Columbus's Mistakes

Clipped to the foot of my hospital bed, an identity card the size of a playing card—an ace, a deuce, or a goddamned joker—could have told the young priest that I was what was left of Corporal Parmenter Dark Cloud and not whoever he'd come to confess or baptize or circumcise; but shrewdly surmising that the truth must be the pee-colored drug solution dripping into my vein, the young priest decided to persist. "You say that you are not Catholic?"

"I'm not Catholic, I'm not Christian, I'm not anything. I'm Indian."

"The Catholic who asked to see me is Indian, My Son."

It felt weird to hear a man my own age calling me his son; but there was something even more weird going on in my mind. I began seeing the pale blond hair as white and began seeing this skinny young man as the priest back home, frail old Father O'Mara. Confused by the piss-hued drug, I wanted to ask Father O'Mara something, but I didn't know what to ask.

The young priest was turning to leave, and to keep him with me until the question I'd forgotten came back, I said, "Father, I confess—I confess that my guts were dangling from my hands, like butchered pigs' guts used to dangle from our old dog's appreciative growl, but I wasn't praying, I have to confess, I was up on my knees trying to keep my guts out of the mud."

The chaplain's pale blue eyes stared intently into my dark eyes. No doubt he was wondering, was this the post-operative patients' ward, or was this the loony bin?

"I mean, I'm not extra smart, like my younger brother, but I think about things," I mumbled on, not really knowing what I'd say next, but still hoping I'd think of what I wanted to ask. "I mean, somebody rolled a hand grenade under my tent—I mean it was the middle of the night and dark as hell after the explosion, and I got up onto my knees and prayed that I hadn't been blinded for good and prayed that I wouldn't get killed—I mean my father tried to kill my brother—I mean our real father, Father," I added, to try to clarify things.

"I don't have much time," he said, looking between the loops of black beads, where an oval wristwatch reposed like the gold head of a snake protected by black coils.

"That's what I mean," I lied, pretending to misunderstand. "Nobody has much time." I felt like I was a little kid again, trying to keep my father beside my bed, for just one more story. "You don't have much time. I don't have much time. Nobody has much time. Not even when they are little kids—Father." To keep the priest beside my bed, where I had to lie most of each day, to rest my not-quite-grown-back-together wounds, I stumbled right on, saying whatever came into my mixed-up mind.

"I was raised by two fathers, Father—one sober and kind and good, one so crazy drunk he'd shoot around his children and scare hell out of them. I thought . . . thought that in war things would be pretty . . . pretty straightforward, I guess. I mean who was supposed to kill who and so on. But, by God, I was fragged, Father. Maybe one of our own soldiers tried to kill me because I'm an Indian, or maybe I'd accidentally machine-gunned one of his buddies. Or he thought I had. I don't know. Nobody knows. What the fuck are we all doing killing and getting killed in a country nobody ever heard of before we invaded? I don't know. Nobody knows. Maybe a Viet Cong sneaked past our guards. Maybe it was some guy we hired to do some of our shit work and we didn't pay him enough—or, hell, maybe he loved his country, and we couldn't have paid him enough. Maybe there isn't enough, in the whole fucking world. I'm damned if I know, but, by God, one thing I do know, I was fragged!"

The priest nodded, wisps of blond hair, which sweat had stuck to his brow, dislodging and slipping down and almost touching his pale, raised eyebrows. "Fragged," he repeated, looking quite pleased, probably because he'd at last heard something familiar, something that would let him start to piece together a logical explanation for my ramblings. "Fragged. Yes. Someone tried to kill you with a fragmentation grenade." With one hand he vigorously patted my hands, which were clutching each other as if in prayer, but actually they were pressed to ease the pain from stitching holding my chest together. "Fragged." The priest smiled. "That's terrible. You have my sympathy."

"Sympathy? No, no, Father, it was another word that nobody ever uses that Father O'Mara used, Father—used one of the days when my father shot at my brother Juke. It wasn't 'sympathy'—no." I could hear my loving mother reminding her know-it-all eldest son that he was supposed to thank this priest for his sympathy, and I mumbled, "Thank you, Father." But I was beginning to feel the question that I wanted to ask—had to ask—slipping away in the effort of just keeping the priest with me; and I thought about trying to keep my intense feeling by saying loving things to prostitutes and calling them by the names of girls I'd wanted, back home. Hearing myself laugh at what I'd only remembered and not said, I felt the same certainty that the priest's pale, narrowing eyes showed—the certainty that I was insane. Not just grunt-soldier crazy, the way all of us had become in order to get through combat and remain more or less human—not just group craziness, but my own real, personal, individual, out-of-control insanity.

It made me mad as hell. At myself. At the priest. At everything.

"God is just," I yelled at the Man of God, "just, goddamn it, not fair."

"What isn't fair, My Son?" His fingers gripped his rosary, as if he was getting ready to whip me across the face because I'd insulted his God. "Be calm, be calm," he said, his voice shaky. "Be calm."

"I'm calm," I shouted at him. "I'm so goddamned chock-full of drugs I can't not be calm."

A lot of patients were moving toward us. "I'm very calm," I said. "I really am. Safe here, in a hospital, and on whatever drug this is, I'm calm, I'm calm."

"That's right, My Son," the chaplain told me, adding his professional manner to what the drug was supposed to be doing for me; but, like the drug, his well-intentioned words also had a side effect.

"It feels queer—it feels very queer—fairy queer your calling me your son," I babbled. I'd just had my shot. "I mean, you're a fairy nice fellah, I'm sure," I said insolently, imitating what I'd heard a drill sergeant tell a delicate recruit, "but you're sure as hell—sure's heck—not my father, Father." The priest shifting his shiny shoes, I tried to keep him talking. "Why don't you call me Brother, Father," I said. "I think 'Brother' would help us keep things straight—I mean about just who the hell we are and so on."

He fidgeted, his body all loose and uncertain, only his white-knuckled hand tense as he gripped the coils of black beads.

The coils around his wristwatch had made me think of a snake, a gold-oval-headed blacksnake with a short black fang and a long black fang and a longer black tongue moving around and around, and when I heard a low buzzing, I thought "rattlesnake." But it was only somebody's electric wheelchair maneuvering between a half a dozen crutch-cane-and-walking-frame-supported patients who hadn't had any recent excitement, other than that on TV. Black cripples and white cripples were all together, an audience, just a pattern of black and white like the priest's priestly vest and collar inside the shell of his green army outer uniform. "Brother. Brothers in Christ," the young Father said brightly—long, Dracula-looking teeth flashing in his pale face. "That's a good idea, My Brother, a good idea." He looked around at the wounded men circling us, and I realized that he was thinking that some of them might be Catholic and concerned about their priest's dignity, and he was winking at each of them, to signal that he was only humoring a crazy nut.

"It has been nice talking to you . . . Brother," he said, and took my hand to shake it and leave—to visit, I remembered, whatever Indian he'd intended to visit before he'd been directed to me by mistake—a Big mistake, he must be thinking.

And he'd just made an even bigger mistake, shaking hands. I gripped hard and wouldn't let go. My grip was still the strong grip of a kid who'd done hard farmwork every day of his life since childhood, even though squeezing a trigger was the hardest work it had done lately.

Wincing from pain, the chaplain looked around, maybe deciding if he should ask—or order, since he was a captain as well as a chaplain—order the other patients to help—help, even though he was the only uninjured man among us. It seemed funny. I heard my loony laugh again and could see the other patients giving me strange—or understanding— looks. Drugged, I couldn't hold back—couldn't stop giggling like a little kid. I let the priest's hand drop, clamped my hand—tasting now of his cigarettes—over my sobbing mouth and gripped my lips down hard against my teeth.

"Sybarite," I remembered, and it wasn't anything I'd meant to get into with this stranger, this priest from a church I'd only visited during weddings and funerals.

"Sybarite?" the young priest asked.

The hand I'd just released joining the other hand in clutching black beads, I heard myself say, in a little kid's anxious-to-please voice, "That's not a snake, from the fucking Garden of Eden, that's a rosary—like the ones my teacher would whip us with. 'Wild Indians,' she called us—even the white kids—when we'd been bad. Out in the bush—out in what my buddies called 'Indian Country,' I saw men do things that were really naughty. You don't dare to object when your buddies are raping and torturing and—and murdering—but you can at least go on thinking about doing the right thing."

"Yes," the young priest said. "Yes, My . . . Son . . . My Brother—thinking is important—very important."

Two orderlies, who had sneaked up either side of my bed, gripped my upper arms. Hard! Just as I'd grabbed the priest's hand. Just as I'd grabbed my own crazy, blabbering mouth. A doctor joined the priest and gave an order. A nurse swabbed my biceps with a cool dab of alcohol-soaked cotton, and a needle struck home.

Consciousness was slipping away; and I felt something—something important—the question I'd wanted to ask—ask the priest, the Man of God, the young Father O'Mara—the question slipping, slipping away.

"I was looking for an Indian who is Catholic," I heard the priest tell his brother officer, the doctor. "And someone directed me to this Indian by mistake."

"All of us Indians are mistakes. That's what they teach us in school," I heard myself mumble. "Old Christopher Columbus was looking for some Asian people for Spaniards to kill and rob, but old Chris found us, and they had to kill and rob us instead."

"There's only one other Indian here, a patient of mine, as a matter of fact—a fellow with one of those mixed Biblical and Indian names—Jukiah Dark Cloud," the psychiatrist said.

"Juke here? My brother, Father? I'll be damned. So he's the other Indian," I heard myself mumble. "He volunteered. He didn't wait to be drafted."

"Oh, the army drafted me, and then the army shafted me," some patient sang.

"I haven't much time left," the chaplain said. "But where will I find the Indian I've been trying to find?"

"That's what I want to ask you," I shouted. "My brother Juke even wrote a poem about it in high school. 'Where can any Vanishing American, like me, find the Native American he used to be?'"

"What? Oh, of course, you want to find your brother, Brother," the chaplain said, getting it all mixed up. "I'll tell him—try to tell him . . . I'm sorry to tell you that he is not well, not well at all—mentally, I mean to say." He paused, probably thinking that craziness must run in the family. "Your brother feels guilty, it seems, for doing things a soldier must do, and I've been called to hear his confession and help him regain the peace of mind he needs to go on doing his duty as a soldier—the peace I need, and the peace you need, My Brother, the peace all of us need."

"I mean," I said, hearing what he'd said but not understanding it. "I mean, 'Sybarite.' I mean what does it mean, Father? Father O'Mara called my father a sybarite, Father, just before my father started shooting—to scare Juke and make him more obedient . . . more, more like me, I guess. I mean, what does it mean? What in hell does anything, anything mean?"

The two orderlies let go of my arms, and I was dimly aware of my hands plopping down onto the mattress; but just before women's screams came up in my mind, obscuring all the sounds of the ward, I heard the priest say clearly, "I don't know."

"I mean I wanted to know—I mean, killing women and children. Do you believe—really believe—in God—God the Father, Father?" I tried to shout before it was too late; but the screams were loud in my head, and I could barely hear the priest continuing: "It's a word that I've never heard. Forgive me."

Maybe I only think I remember his saying, Forgive me. But whether he'd said it or I'd only needed to believe he'd said it, I felt that I would not ever forgive him, and not forgive my father—and not forgive my goddamned war-crazy nation—and not forgive the killer I'd become.

# A Handprint in Columbus's Homeland's Dust

"Juke, my so-called Four Freedoms War, it weren't all snappy uniforms and flags," my father told me, after I'd said that I'd earn a college education by fighting in Vietnam, and this will be Dad's story, his voice in my words—a bad telephone connection maybe, but the only one.

"They was just kids, eighteen or so, no older'n you are now, them soldiers I'd been ordered to kill before they could tell some old offysir where to aim his big guns to stop our side's attack."

"It was a last-month's bomb crater the two kids had picked for their observation post, a good place, and naturally the first I chose to climb a tree on a hill and aim my tellyscope-sight down into.

"Twigs was stuck in nets covering those little soup-bowl helmets the boys wore; but blobs and curlycues and squiggly shapes on brand new uniforms was as bright as what you kids used to make in school with them finger-paint sets, and the cammyflodge wasn't doing much cammyflodgin'.

"Back where I'd started from, our soldiers was stacking up artillery shells like farmers stacking bags of oats for a long day's planting, and back where these two kids' microphone connected with earphones, there would be stacks and stacks of artillery shells hidden under nets with leafy branches stuck in them, to fool our airplanes. "All hell was ready to bust loose, but it was quiet where I was and where the two Italian observers was—quiet, except for birds warning each other about those jibber-jabbering, school-boy soldiers, who outnumbered me two to one, like our side would outnumber theirs once the big battle really started. For a sniper like me off by his lonesome, more numbers just meant more targets.

"I shot the one, and the other he kind of automatically put out a hand to his friend. I shot again, and the hand, it fell. It just fell. By the time I'd shinnied on down from the tree and run on over to make sure of things, the first kid's blood had brimmed a vivid, sunshiny red around the second kid's hand inside the little dust dike the hand had throwed up when it dropped.

"It seemed kind of pitiful, even young and ignorant as I was then, and even after all I'd seen happen and done and all I'd just barely managed to keep from happening to me—pitiful, that skinny, Indniun-looking, Italian-brown hand reaching out, with no thinking, no time to think—just reaching out, just reaching out towards the dying friend—and then, just to fall.

"Blood was holding on to itself for dear life; and even though it was higher than dirt flared up around the fallen hand, none wasn't spilling over. Lucky for me I didn't wait around for when it would spill, because I'd smashed the radio and busted the eardrums of some old enemy offysir. He must of been royally pissed off, and there was one little hill he had on his map very accurate.

"If I hadn't already run like hell down into the first thick stand of trees, there would have been three body-size containers of blood emptying into that old last-month's battle's bomb crater. And that would have been, as we used to say, 'All she wrote.' All she wrote. For me. My last day. You not yet even a gleam in my and your mother's eyes. No kids that I could call my own, so far as I knew, nobody to carry me on, nobody. Nobody. *All she wrote.* Instead, I scrunched down into the moldy leaves of ever so many seasons and heard the shrapnel chopping a hundred winters' supply of wood above me.

"As soon as that old offysir out across those Italian miles stopped his artillery from wasting shells on cutting wood around one scared Indniun, I took out lickety-split for another part of the world.

"My wristwatch showed plenty of time to get to the other side of our own artillery barrage, and up to then, I hadn't encountered any enemy patrols. It should have been all OK, and me back with a few minutes to spare to tell our colonel exactly where the observation post had been, and to let him start figuring out how the choice of that particular piece of high ground might connect with a map pattern of high-ground places and what the last air-reconnaissance pictures had showed, or whatever—just a short while and my job ought to have been done and my blood still where it was meant to be and as safe as red wine jugged in a sand-bagged cellar.

"The hell of it was that when the old enemy artillery offysir had wasted some of his cannon shells, why then our side's old artillery offysir, he took it kind of personal and decided to let go with a few rounds, even though he was supposed to be saving the ammunition to concentrate a barrage ahead of our attack. He thought the enemy shells had either killed me or they hadn't, and a few more shells from our side wouldn't make that much difference, he said. It was damned nice of him, really, to explain, considering I was just a corporal and he didn't have to tell me nothing.

"So there I was, up on my two feet, like a human being for a change, chancing an enemy patrol so's I could make some speed and get back ahead of our artillery barrage, when, sweet Jesus, here it comes ahead of time, explosions flashing and flaring like lightning in a dark storm back t'home, and believe me, I was plenty content to go down on my belly to crawl like a worm. Our old artillery offysir's 'brief retaliatory reply' got sent to the wrong party. Holy Christ, there was enough wood-chopping to take care of all the winters left before Judgment Day. If they'd of give me a Purple Heart ribbon for every wound left by a wood splinter, the chest of my dress uniform would of looked like chickenpox.

"I told myself 'Your ass is grass,' as the black troops in the labor battalion that dug our gun pits used to say—'You-urr a-uss is gra-uss'—but I scrunched into the moldy leaves as deep as I could, even if I couldn't help thinking the soft stuff my bare hands could dig would do damned little to stop what was chopping hard oak up above me. I did a little praying. I did more than a little praying. I sent up to the heavens some Christian-type prayers the chaplains had been training us with. And down into The Sacred Earth, I sent some Cherokee prayers I'd heard my mother say—not in the old language, which she never knew none of, but in English—and all of my whole trembling body was sending one prayer: Please, Lord God, Please, Great Spirit, please save me. The explosions stopped, no thanks to my prayers, I guess, but because our artillery offysir was saving the rest of his fireworks for the real battle. It had been what they called a walking barrage, only running to beat hell was more like it, and after it had stomped on over me, I started to rise from the moldy-leaf dike my body had raised, plopping itself prone. My meat was a kind of dike itself, with its red rivers and cricks and lakes and trickles held in, I can think now; but I didn't do no such thinking then, because my damned-near-beat-to-death eardrums heard the sound of pounding feet.

"Knowing there was nobody from our side out there but me, I sank back down deep into tree fertilizer, and remembering the two enemy kids' cammyflodge uniforms they hadn't finished cammyflodging with mud, I was hoping my own dirty cammyflodge looked like past seasons' dropped and dead and near-rotted leaves, with some just-blowed-off green leaves mixed in.

"Following the old tree cutter's lane I'd got off of in order to plop down out of sight, a dozen soldiers run on past. Like me, those Italians wanted to be someplace else when and if a P.S. was added to the not-so-goddamned-brief retaliatory reply our artillery offysir had sent to their artillery offysir.

"As soon as I couldn't hear boots pounding ground anymore, I jumped on up and started running pell-mell, because my watch showed maybe—only just maybe—enough time to get across a plowed field and back into the woods, which hid our troops.

"I had me this feeling, as my mother used to say, that I wasn't going to make it, and like most old Indniun superstition feelings, mine was right.

"When the American shells started exploding to start our attack, I made for the only farmyard in that particular part of God's Creation and ran straight to the wine cellar, because I knew those stone walls and packed clay would protect me from anything except a direct hit, and I also knew no artilleryman was going to intentionally zero in on wine.

"What I didn't know was that some of the Italian patrol had done the same human thinking I had done. Because I'd flung open the heavy plank door and dived in in a rush, letting the door bang down, their candle went out, shutting us all in darkness.

"'Luigi?' someone hollered over the sound of the shells beating hell out of the barn and the farm house, and when I hollered back one name I knew from the newspapers, Mussolini's first name, 'Benito,' everybody sent a whole day's worth of jubilation into my ears. Somebody hugged me and slobbered a wet, whiskery kiss on where he'd last seen my whiskery, Italian-looking, Indniun-brown cheek, and got me square on my big, hatchet-blade Indniun nose. Then, somebody put a wine bottle into my hand in the dark.

"That first drink I took might of been the longest any human ever had on this earth, because while I was making that big wine bottle gurgle, I didn't have to try to talk. The lucky thing was that those Italians were, like me, all a lot more interested in drinking than talking, especially since one guy would only get about two jibber-jabber words out when another artillery shell would finish the sentence for him.

"We had been directing the bottles around by Braille, so to speak, and glugging and slurping away for quite some time when all to the once I felt some little tugs and pats on my rifle.

"I had to hold down my urge to pull away and start shooting, but the rifle wouldn't have been much use to me at close quarters in the dark. I took another big snort of wine. It was new-made, the smell and the taste of their dark red, almost black, grapes still in it.

"I made the drink a especially long one, because it might possibly be my last good thing on earth, and then, since nobody had reached out to touch my arm, wanting his turn at the bottle, I took another long drink.

"The plank door was all the time rattling like all the troops waiting to kill each other were knocking to be let in to join the drinking instead, and every shell that landed made the wine bottle shake in my fingers and made my rifle barrel quiver, even though there was me and somebody else a holding onto it.

"When the candle it got lit again, I took a quick drink to put the big bottle up in front of my face; but even as I did this, I saw that two of the Italians had their hands closed around my gun barrel, making sure that it would stay aimed at the wine-cellar ceiling. I figured my ass was grass, because there was damned little chance that four enemies about to have to run like hell for their lives would trouble to take a prisoner.

"But they were grinning at me, all four of them.

"'I know you,' one of them said, giving a drunk, foreign-sounding chortle but speaking English more or less. 'I know you, because I smile you rifle is been shoot, and who did we shoot? Nobody. Nobody. I think those two boys. How to know? I smile you rifle, is it stink like it been shoot.'

"They were all showing purple-wine-stained white teeth in their dark, Indniun-looking faces in the candlelight flickers, all drunk as skunks and all admiring the wisdom of the one who'd smelled my gun in the dark.

"They all smelled the rifle, passing it back and forth so casually, so close to me I almost believed they were going to give it back; and when they gave me one of their rifles to feel how light it was, I realized that now the candle was lit, I could try to shoot my way out of the fix I was in. But damn it, the rifle they'd handed me it wasn't even a semiautomatic like mine, but just a old slow bolt action gun, and anyway, we'd all been through an artillery barrage together and drinking together, and what the hell, by then I was probably feeling the wine.

"'Sal-oo-tay,' I said, as I'd learned to say in their drinking places we'd already captured.

"'Cheers,' the rifle smeller said, and we all five had another round of drinks.

"I was snoring, fast asleep, just like my four captors, when our soldiers followed up the artillery barrage and, in capturing the wine cellar's few full and several empty bottles, captured me along with my drinking buddies. Suspicious at seeing five dark-complexioned faces, the sergeant wouldn't let me carry my rifle until he'd emptied it.

"By the time a private with a loaded rifle had marched me and the four Italians through two Military Police control points, I'd sobered and was speaking English a lot more clear. At the third checkpoint, I just said 'Corporal Dark Cloud and Private whatever-his-name-was delivering four prisoners,' and Private whatever-his-name-was heard 'Corporal' and tried to remember if he had really been told to keep me under guard.

"He didn't look doubtful again until we reached a barbed-wire stockade and the four enemies all kissed me on both whiskery, mud-cammyflodged cheeks before the gate swung shut.

"'I guess they're happy I never shot them when I had the chance,' I told the private, and shrugged.

"He shrugged back.

"'Rejoin your unit, Private,' I told him. I was a corporal.

"I was a corporal, and one of our offysirs, he ordered me to march a dozen scared new troops forward, through gun smoke and fog so thick we could only just barely see each other, hunched in the cold and miserable and gray—and see whatever else was close. Even in fog, I knew this piece of earth better'n I'd ever wanted to. We marched, me and them kids, trees gray, and the grass gray, and the dead soldiers gray, like logs covered with mold. We marched past the wine cellar, its plank door wide open now, showing only empty bottles. We marched over the little hill with the two heaps of meat lying side by side and covered by dew as scummy as toads' eggs.

"Juke, they already got your brother over there, fighting in this Veet-nam, and you, you damned young fool, go on up to Canada, like a lot of your friends has done. Stay to hell out of this war what's got nothing to do with you and not no Indniun whatever was."

For the first and only time in my life, I saw a bayonet-scarred, work-scarred hand wiping tears from gray-whiskered cheeks, and I reached out, just like the little kid I'd been, begging one more story, please, please, just one more, one more, wanting, now, understanding and love.

Dad shut black-lashed, wet lids down tight, maybe feeling the pain he had endured and, through me, would have to endure again. When he shook off my hand, it fell, it just fell, and persuaded by pronouncements about democracy and by promises of a chance to go to college, I hitchhiked away from my old soldier father and into his youth.

# A Vanishing American and the War Between the States

I had one advantage over the other soldiers, Dad. You'd got me used to being shot at and not knowing why. "Sergeant Jukiah Dark Cloud sustained wounds due to enemy action," my citation read, but really, an American helicopter rocketed an American truck that I'd been trying to reach before it blew up in my face. The pilot had done me a major favor, because my year's tour of duty in what whites called Indian Country ended while I was recovering.

I got a pass from the hospital, and I was coming back from—well, hell, you were a soldier, Dad—a whorehouse. I felt pretty good after having had a . . . blow-job, we called it, from this sort of good-looking, slender woman—more or less my age, I guess, not really much more than a high school girl, in case they ever had a high school in that part of the world. Oral sex was what the medical officers had said I had to have—because anything any more athletic might tear open the stitching they'd done after cutting out shrapnel.

I was hoping for a good night's sleep, but about half a step into the ward, ninety miles per hour, right in my face, here comes a piece of metal the size of a meat cleaver blade. As I flinched sideways, an edge, sharp enough to split my skull, caught the peak of my go-to-hell cap and turned the damned cap around all galley-west and crooked, then sliced air past my ear and ended up with one corner stabbed into the door I'd just closed.

"What the fuck?" I yelled. I was ready to fight. I mean, I wasn't ready for any fight—was too damned weak even to climb on top of a whore, and it hurt still just to slowly walk—but I was pulling my goddamned belt out of its loops, the one thing I had that would serve as a weapon—except for my boots, and I was in no shape for launching any kicks.

I'd have had my dark, Indian face—and my white-thinking brain— split right down the middle if I hadn't swerved my head, but I was too deranged to turn around and get the hell out of there. I mean, I'd thought I was more or less safe in the hospital, where I'd been brought back to life after damned near bleeding to death. What would you have thought, Dad? What did you think during those drunk-out-of-your-mind times of trying to hold your own against drunk-out-of-their-minds white veterans in Custer's Bottomless Keg? I thought, Some son of a bitch is trying to kill me again.

Actually, I'd stumbled into a melee of patients, some not able to get out of bed but able to throw things, some leaning against walls and battling with crutches, some fist-fighting the best they could from wheelchairs, and some on the floor, hardly able to see and groping around to find broken medicine bottles and leave somebody else as blind as a bat.

It took me a few drunken moments to figure out that I was in the middle of the goddamndest race riot I'd ever seen. The steel plate had been intended to split the head of somebody else. I should have felt relieved. But no. Maybe it was Mom's tooth-for-tooth, eye-for-eye religion, or maybe, like the psychiatrist said, Dad, I was permanently pissed off about your shooting and splintering floor around my feet when I was little. I don't know why, but I felt that, by God, I was going to make somebody sorry he'd thrown that goddamned sharp-edged, heavy steel, which had been, till then, the hospital's make-do dustpan.

I went limping right into the ruckus, and all of the black guys and all of the white guys stopped slugging away at one another's bandaged flesh and just stared at this crazy latecomer, with his uniform unrumpled and his go-to-hell cap twisted around crooked on his black Indian hair. Maybe they thought I was a goddamned military policeman whose armband had been torn off. Whatever.

"Who the fuck threw that goddamned steel?" I yelled, my belt wrapped around my right fist—your razor strop stinging my little butt, Dad, and shriveling my little ego, Dad, inside my brain.

It might have been like that in England's old days. Two kings or princes or barons yell, Put your goddamned swords away, you unworthy lackeys, and the two of us splendid gentlemen will fight to see who gets to go home with the other's flag or crown—or whatever they were all hacking each other apart to win.

"I'm sorry, Sarge," a small red-haired guy told me, looking up into my crazy eyes, and I think it was my craziness more than my sergeant stripes that had gotten his respect. He'd no doubt been crazy like that himself, and he hadn't ended up in a fucking wheelchair by slipping on a banana peel. "I didn't throw at you, he said. "I threw at . . ." He looked around the dozen or so black guys—and he wasn't just being careful not to start things up again, I could see he wasn't; I could see that he honestly didn't know who the hell he had tried to kill and had almost killed me by mistake. "I'm sorry, buddy," he said—he didn't say "Sarge"—and then he laughed one of those crazy laughs like you'd hear a lot in the wards. And he said—not to me, and not to the white guys around him or the black guys bunched on the other side of the aisle, and not to himself—he just said out into the medicine-smelling air of the ward, "We was bullshitting each other about the Civil War and Northerners and Southerners and white guys and black guys, and then we started fighting, and I don't even know what the fuck we were fighting about."

Then everybody started pointing at my stupid-looking little go-to-hell cap turned around on my unharmed head, all of them laughing, as crazy as bedbugs. My rage vanished; and my being a Vanishing American in a black-and-white world vanished. I was a crazy man among crazy men, all of us giggling like little kids, all of us crazy and happy just because we were alive, and yes, Dad, you had some right to your own craziness, and I forgive you for getting drunk and shooting around my little feet a few times, and past my little head, I tell him—don't tell him, can't—he's dead, whatever that means. He's easier to talk to this way, but—just like the world's crazy nations, fighting and then making up—it's too damned late to do any good.

# Some Killings, One Accidental

I got out of her car, but this time she didn't say she'd pick me up tomorrow.

Her brake lights flashed through trees at the bottom of the hill, and a long time later, a light went on in a house across the river.

Next night, the foreman asked, "Your squaw go back to the reservation or what?"

When he went into the office, I sort of swept the floor in that direction and heard him tell the night manager, "Screw her, we'll mail her her check to her; she can damned well get herself on down here and get her her own check herself, not even giving us notice we'd have to hire a replacement." But the night manager shook his head, no, he'd have to mail the check, so I guessed that I'd never see her again.

"You want a ride back to town?" she asked that first time, and I got in.

"Why don't the other men ever give you a lift?" she asked. I didn't know.

"Because you're Indian," she guessed, starting the engine and turning on the headlights.

"My husband's friends at the university say you're crazy. Are you?" she asked after a while, and when I didn't answer, she said, "You're studying mathematics, they say.

"They say the Veterans' Office got you this job, and you'll spend the rest of your life as a janitor. But still you're able to pass university courses? "You're light-skinned, maybe a quarter Indian, and I'm half Lakota, from my dad's side of the family, not one of these Wannabe Indians from a hippie commune."

After a while, she asked where I lived. I pointed.

"I'm married, to a psychologist, and I'm twenty-six, but I can't believe the obscenity of those men we work with," she said.

Black hair braided back at the nape, as the foreman had ordered— "Or else'n them mean old machines might rip off your pretty, pretty scalp"—she looked sixteen, the age of my father's mother's mother, kidnapped and taken to learn white language and religion, thin face scared but defiant in the photo.

"I have two kids and a husband to support through this last year of his doctorate. Not being able to tell him anything makes it worse," she told me, talking faster as the car slowed. "I'm real glad we're married and all, but he's white, and he doesn't know what it's like, being a woman and being Indian. Thanks for letting me talk," she said.

I guess my white mother's first husband was Lakota, and he was killed in the war my Cherokee father survived.

"I'll pick you up on my way to work tomorrow night," the Lakota woman said.

Next night her car stopped beside me on the bridge.

"Hey, I went to pick you up like I said," she said, "but no one answered your doorbell. Get in."

I got in.

"Tomorrow night you wait for me," she said. "I'll pick you up at your room."

Next night she found me just before I got to the bridge.

"Get in," she said. "Indians should help one another. I want to help you." I got in.

"I see you riding home with the squaw," the foreman says. "It's good to get a ride, huh? Good to get a ride?"

I'm playing pool with him against two machine operators, just for fun. Sometimes we make money, playing guys who don't know us.

"There's our eight ball as black as a nigger's tit," the foreman says.

Two black men stride over, pool cues' heavy ends up.

"What's that about 'nigger'?" one of them asks.

"Tonto here, he said it," the foreman says.

The two black men are bigger than I am, but they take in the size of my shoulders and arms and the wrist scars I maybe got from somebody's knife in a bar, or in a bayonet fight, or when my wife left me. They look at each other and go back to their own game.

I want to miss the eight ball, but I can't. I slide the pool cue. It stops, the blue tip quivering slightly above bright green felt. The white ball clicks against the black, and the black ball drops into shadows.

"I think I'll have me that nigger whore again and give the wife a little vacation tonight," the foreman says very loud.

The old woman who runs the whorehouse says, "This 'Black is Beautiful' talk made my Negro girl go straight."

"All cats are the same color at night," the foreman snickers. "That little young spic I had last time, she'll do."

"They won't leave me alone," the Lakota woman said. "I tried joking them out of it, like my husband said. I tried to shame them, talking about my kids. I went to the night manager, but he just said, 'There was never any trouble till these so-called Equality laws made us hire you,' and looked me over himself."

The moon, reflected below the dam, exploded into foam as white as smoke from huts I had to torch in Vietnam. Then, the car accelerating beyond the bridge, ripples glittered like rows of molten gold numbers, in dreams.

"Maybe you could sort of stand up for me," the Lakota woman said, "like a brother."

After a while she said, "You don't even stand up for yourself, do you. You're strong. You could. But you don't, do you? They bedevil you and throw all their dirty jobs your way and throw their lunch scraps on the floor just to make it nastier for you to sweep. Myself—I'm outnumbered. I'm trapped by my need for money to support my children—but I'm no more a victim than you are, am I?"

"She loves it, if truth was known," the old warehouse chief is saying to his assistant. "Her husband's a fruit who ain't found it out himself quite yet, most likely, like all of these young longhair university fellers are these days. Or half of them anyways are half that way, at least, that's what this doctor says in some magazine or on TV . . . anyhow a real doctor—for the head I mean."

A commotion has moved over near the little glass-enclosed office at the far corner of the huge production room. Voices rise above the noises of the machines, then sink, then rise and sink again, like the cries of a buddy losing his grip on a rifle barrel I held out to him, and sinking and coming up, his yelling fading as he plunged downstream, trying to get rid of his pack and fighting for air, then sinking again. The two warehouse men are staring toward the office, their heads, one gray, one blond, cheek to cheek in the narrow opening of the huge storage-room door. The door is heavy, and they don't open it any more than they have to when I press the buzzer that there's another huge spool of paper needed for a machine or a waste-paper bale to go out onto the loading dock. They'll make me push the door open the rest of the way for them. They do it every time. The old warehouse man calls me Sampson. He tells me to open the door one-handed. I do. He tells me to shove it open with my left hand. Sometimes near the end of the night I cannot do it and have to use both hands, even though I can always open the door with just my right hand if I haven't failed with my left hand first. It's like it used to be when I was able to do things—play football, get married, do things—and then, if I remembered I was Indian and everything had always been hopeless, ever since I'd been born, I couldn't do anything.

"It ain't that he's a Indniun he's so strong for the size he is, it's cause he's touched in the head," the old warehouse man tells every new assistant. "Parm here, he was not no stronger than you or me till something in Vietnam blew his brain loose."

June bugs are hurling their hard shells against the bright bulb behind the two men, the sound like some guy flipping his finger against a beer glass, getting himself worked up to fight.

Lit by the bulb, a calendar girl is gowned in white, breasts naked between wide-flung bridal-gown lapels, not too obviously thrust out or coyly half withdrawn. Face framed by hair glistening black like the earth she knows must cover her soon, she is not the blond cheerleader I married before I was drafted and sent to war.

"He's hell on wheels in the whorehouse," the warehouse chief tells each new assistant. "Not bad looking, for a Indniun, and he's got a cock as big as a mule's. They love that. A whore, you know, she loses half the feeling in her cunt, at least half, and it takes a telephone pole to remind her what a cock used to be. The girls are scared, him being half crazy and not saying nothing; but scared or not, if it was them to choose, it'd be him every time."

My wife divorced me while I was still in the hospital and not able to notice things, I think, but can't be sure.

"Looks like the guys been diddling the little squaw again," the old warehouse chief says. "But I guess it's all over now. The night manager has her in the office. Maybe she's going to quit. Good riddance. Can't take a little fooling around, the stuck-up Indniun bitch. Husband's at the university. Half queer, so I understand. Maybe you know him."

"No," the assistant says, making his voice deeper than it is. "So many of us students up there nobody knows anybody."

He looks at the order sheet I'd handed him and gets onto the loading machine.

"Probably a fruit himself and stuck-up," the old warehouse man tells me. "Won't hire him back once the freight car gets unloaded. Hates to hear me talking about your squaw. All that damned education us taxpayers pays for—probably you was stuck-up, too, when you had all your marbles. Christ! I'd like to make you say something just once.

"Maybe you think, all tanned right down to her tits, the June bride here looks Indniun." He shoves a finger toward the calendar girl.

"Not that stack!" he shouts, although he hasn't looked away from the calendar—just knows from the sound where the lifting machine has stopped. He has the whole huge warehouse inside his head: grades of paper, weights of paper, rag content of paper. "That fruit-cake college boy couldn't find his prick using both hands."

Behind me there's another commotion rising above the steady surge of the machines.

Skin glowing in the niche where white routing slips are impaled on a glistening spike, the June woman is tanned dark like a Madonna painting I saw in Vietnam, one breast bare, the infant Christ deeply intent on human milk.

"At least the manager finally knew he had to do something, and I can keep my job." The Lakota woman is crying hard, her car veering so sometimes I see headlights in the river. "Jesus! What kind of country is this where men can half undress a woman because she needs to work to support her husband and kids."

She has turned onto the street where I see her car lights disappearing every dawn, and we are going uphill. After a block or so, she discovers this herself.

"Oh, God, I'm sorry. I'm so damned mad, I was taking you to my home, and you weren't even going to tell me, were you? You were just going to walk on back. Christ, I've been acting like you don't even exist. Just like those men treat you—and me . . . have treated me. Parm, the manager knew he had to do something or see five of his trained pressmen in city jail. And you—you don't have to take any more abuse. You must realize that now, even if you are a little—well, they say crazy. Why not? My husband says we're all a little crazy, and he's a psychologist—or he will be. Those men were crazy to think they could get away with taking off my shirt. Now the bottom-pinching and the obscenities are going to stop, too. This goddamned country. When I was studying in England, they arrested a drunk just because he was staring at girls on a bus—and the girls were in miniskirts even—but just for staring. I had rights there. I was a person there. But here—those goddamned filthy—those . . .

"Don't take it anymore, Parm. You're Indian, just like I am. This is our land, and we should be proud. You fought for this brutal country in Vietnam, and look what it did to you. You should fight for yourself, and you should fight for our people. You shouldn't take abuse." She parks in front of the stair that goes to my room.

"Oh God I've been telling you my troubles again, she says, and the troubles you've got, I should complain. But I feel so much better having told you. Parm, I feel so sorry for you. I hope I'm not being bad for what's inside you. They say your wife left you while you were in the army hospital. They say she was pretty and white and only married you because you were a high school football star—some classmates my husband met in the graduate-student lounge said so, I mean."

Because of her driving very slowly, it is dawn, air from the river fresh, cardinals flashing past, as orange as orioles in the early light. Her wet face and eyes are glowing. A dove, close, is talking to others far away. And I can almost remember something I want to remember, not just what comes.

When I was a child, I had to lie awake in darkness and hear my father's drunken threats and fists and my mother's sobs. In Vietnam, I had to keep my mouth shut while men did terrible things to women.

"I'm sorry," I hear a man's voice say. It's me. Talking.

She grabs my shoulders and cries so long my T-shirt soaks through, and my chest-hair follicles smart with salt from her tears. We climb the stairs to where I sleep, and I move as I am beginning to remember once moving, slow, to hear between steps the sounds of small feet moving in rhythm with mine. She only wants me to hold her, and I hold her. When I wake up, she's gone. Everyone goes. They go or they die. No one stays.

"A society as crazy as ours has got to penalize any insanity that's not our own codified craziness," the little priest said. "We send you to Vietnam and give you three medals for killing complete strangers. You come back so traumatized that you're judged to be mentally disabled, but then society says you're sane enough to be executed for killing an old man—even though it seems you killed him for nothing more than tearing the leaf off a calendar. Maybe they're right. Maybe you are crazier than the rest of us. Why didn't you kill a general? Or the president? Why did you kill an old guy who'd have been dead in a few years anyhow?"

His black clothes had vanished into shadows, and above the white collar, his face was very innocent and tired.

"A masters degree in higher mathematics nearly completed, and the only job you could or would keep was janitor work. A strong athletic body and you let anyone bully you. Young, a handsome face, and your only love life after your wife divorced you was whores. Hearing all your lawyer said on TV yesterday, I could almost believe in the vanity of everything human and become a conventional Christian again." He laughed—the thin, crazy laugh of salesmen when they've been too long saying what they don't believe.

It was good of him to stay with me all night, and I wanted to be nice to him, but I hoped he'd leave before dawn.

"I wish I could help you," he said, "to at least understand why you are being executed. Was it that courageous woman who lost her husband for trying to save you at your trial? After the others de-escalated to giving her what they called the silent treatment, did the old warehouse man say something about her—one insult too many? Did the other men's destructive silence toward her remind you of your own silence, your sins of omission?"

The priest wanted facts. He wanted to help me, and he thought that facts would do the job.

"Left-handed," the old warehouse man had said. He'd been bawled out for insulting the young black man who'd just been hired to take the Lakota woman's place, and now, he needed to boss me around.

The huge warehouse was still all shadows, columns of printing paper, spool on spool, going up and up into a darkness. The tall, cylindrical columns of paper the plant would convert to business forms for industry all over the world—those columns of paper seemed like the cathedral columns I'd seen in San Francisco, on my way to Vietnam.

"Left-handed, you crazy bastard. What's been bothering you, Parm? You missing your squaw? She remind you of your wife? You just can't hang onto a woman, can you, Parm." He got a crafty look on his wrinkled face. "You young guys thinks us old guys aren't up to much of anything, but I bet you pretend crazy because you ain't no good with women and can say it's because you ain't quite right in the head you can't make it with nothing but a whore."

He knew where I was looking, even though his back was to the calendar, and he turned to shove one finger at the unbuttoned bridal gown and at the face, tranquil and beautiful, above numbers.

"You want to take the June bride home with you, Parm?" the old man asked. "You like to have you a paper dolly, because your Indniun woman was diddled before your eyes, then got phone calls about her kids until she quit?"

I backed away. To get added force from a run. Maybe he thought I was refusing to shut the door—the first time I ever had. I was already lunging when I heard him say, "June's damned near over. You want her. She's yours."

A ball of glossy paper came spinning into the machine-room light, and just before my left hand slammed against the door latch, I saw, too late, the malicious then terrified old face thrust out.

"He killed himself, he didn't mean to. Go! Please go! It's almost dawn."

The little priest looked at me as he had at the first of last night—afraid of a crazy man—mastering his fear, then getting used to me—not even startled when he awoke from dozing.

"It doesn't matter," he said, "whether the old man killed himself or not. You should be in a mental ward. The governor knows that, but he's trailing in the polls, you know. No, I guess you wouldn't know. Anyway, last election you let his opponent put you on TV with other veterans protesting the war. Right-wing voters want to see a redskin peacenik crucified."

When I walked toward the little priest to push him out the door, he said, "Maybe it'll help you accept your fate if you try thinking that you deserve execution for what you did in Vietnam."

I took a step closer, hoping he'd be frightened enough to leave. Instead, he walked back to the chair he'd sat in all night.

"Your soul—" he'd started to say just before I grabbed him.

All night, the guard had been silent in a corner, to let the priest try to comfort me. Unlocking the cell and setting off an alarm, he fled, yelling, "Don't worry, Father, we'll save you," and slammed the door shut just as I tried to fling the priest, still trying to grab me, or to grab anything more solid than air, out.

Fingers crushed, the poor man screamed, and as guards carried him away, he went on screaming, just like the old warehouse man, just like my buddy with his guts twisted around barbed wire, and the enemy searching the darkness for someone to torture and interrogate. I couldn't leave my buddy. I put my fingers around his throat, very gently, then squeezed hard, to end his pain. It was slow, but a shot would have let the enemy know that I was alive. It was the only way. The priest was the first man to tell me the truth—the truth I knew before doors and windows in my head slammed shut, the truth I'd known, and started to forget, the day I was born. Like everyone else alive, I deserve to die. I sent many people into the Spirit Land, but I only knew that gunfire—from jungle, rice-paddy, village—had stopped. "Count bodies," officers ordered, but most of us glanced into hooches we'd "searched" by exploding grenades, then said a high number before setting thatching ablaze.

It is time. I have no watch. But I know.

It is quiet, almost dawn, the air fresh, my fingers on the concrete window ledge as pink as those of a young child.

There are factory whistles. There are cars. People going to work. There are airplanes warming up, bombers preparing to take off, to fly. All is as I remember its being for all of my life. All is far away.

It is dawn, and they will come for me. A European tradition, very old. Brought to the New World. I have said my dawn prayers, and it is time. Against blue dawn sky, another prison wing's window bars are glowing like rows of molten gold numbers. Birds are flying. Cardinals? Orioles? Doves? I cannot tell. They are all black with distance. But they are flying and my mind is flowing—flowing with the minds of my people, my Indian people and my white people, my thoughts like the chunks off ice north of here, floating down a river, floating to the south, to melt, to evaporate into clouds, and to fall, as rain, as snow.

# The Miracle Killing

"A miracle the little boy's alive," the head nurse told student nurses, and the janitor, Juke Dark Cloud, heard, "A miracle. A miracle this man's alive," in an army nurse's voice inside his head.

Harelip a pink worm writhing above white coffee-cup rim, the head nurse continued, "That big car wheel didn't break a single bone, the snow so soft, but of course it was the glare of sun off snow that had prevented the little boy's being seen."

"Here in the chapel, is this where you've been keeping out of sight all morning?" the head nurse had asked Juke, the all-but-invisible Vanishing American.

"Mourning," the hospital chaplain had told his Native American aspirant to Christian belief. "Religion's a vehicle for mourning. This isn't the age of miracles. A congregation-friendly church, that's Christianity today."

Mourning. Buddies just ashes to send, in a flag-wrapped coffin, home—their vehicle a funeral pyre, the rocket "friendly fire."

"Your need for religious solace, that I understand; but you are supposed to be mopping floors, not praying. It's a miracle I found you."

A miracle. Come to count enemy dead, an American patrol had found a nearly obliterated American truck and one Native American, unconscious but blowing bubbles, trying not to drown in his own blood. A miracle. A miracle he wasn't fired already. The kind head nurse his miracle, his harelipped, overweight guardian angel.

"And yesterday—just what did you think you were doing up there outside the operating-rooms?"

Doing? Trying to pray. Up there, where the walls are all windows. Up there, where there's sky, just sky—no hole in the ozone layer, widening to let everybody fry, no napalm bombs, no helicopter rockets, only sky, an infinity of sky, like everywhere in the Old Time, like everywhere. Up there. In the corridor, outside the operating room. Where they save lives. Or can't.

Doing? "Just taking a walk instead of morning coffee." Mourning. "And I didn't know"—that the helicopter pilot had the wrong map, wrong target—"it was over"—the war—"the coffee break"—"a break"—my job, my fiancée, her mind, my fault, my buddies, my fault, my fault, my fault—"a break, please, just one more break."

"I know that adjusting takes awhile," the head nurse decided, "but, Juke, you're lucky it's me again, and not the director. You've got to stop going where you're not supposed to be."

Not on ancestral hunting grounds instead of on the reservation. And not in Asia, the ancestral Indian homeland.

"One more incident, and I'll have to have you fired."

Not fired yet—a miracle—and, another coffee break ended, he pushed the mop cart toward the maternity ward.

"I love you, of course," the sixteen-year-old girl was saying to her twenty-some-year-old boyfriend, saying it loud over the television preoccupation of her thirty roommates, none of whom had a visitor, all of whom half lay, half sat, propped to view the television screen, their bellies a row of graves, mounded under snow.

"I love you, too, a bushel and a peck and a hug around the neck," the boyfriend said, "but you signed up to give away our baby."

"Juke, I—Tap—Love—Taptap—you—and after you're back from Vietnam, maybe, but not now . . . this baby . . . my cousin knows some medical student—almost a doctor."

Tap. The cleaning-solution bottle as heavy as a sledgehammer.

Tap. The foetuses and their shattered glass wombs settled, turning the dust of their shelf to mud, and the nine-months baby fell off its shelf in a sluice of pickling juice, the baby the size of a salmon smashed back by seething cataract—the salmon rotting, bereft of regeneration, except in congregation-unfriendly Nature's plan of Dissolution and Reconstitution—in a logged land's mud-clogged stream—jars' shards glints of ice. I. Love. Tap. Love-tap. You.

"I warned you, earlier today, Juke, that that time had to be the end of it." The end of the day. Of the war. Of love. Tap. Of love. Tap. My girl, her mind, my fault, my buddies, my fault, my fault, my fault. The end of it—the ozone layer—the nuclear age—life. The end of it. Tap. The split pelvis and its long-rooted penis the color of army khaki—the color of bodies cooked inside their truck—formaldehyde's smell the ghosts of buddies, digging graves in membranes of the nose.

"I must say that you picked a good hiding place, Juke. Nobody ever comes in here except the anatomy classes in the fall." Be careful not to make them fall—except in the mind—except from their shadowy shelf in the shadowy mind. "But, Juke, you *have* been working, haven't you? My, how clear those jars are now that you've wiped away the dust. Oh, those unborn babies. I can hardly bear to look. Poor little things. How did you get here anyway?"

"The same way they did."

"What? Oh. But why in the world did you come to the Specimen Room?"

To bring them back into the world, to bury them, to pray for them—to think about burying them—in the world, in the world, in the world.

The head nurse's white face and white-uniformed bulk cast a black shadow as she backed onto pale hallway tile. "Well, Juke, back to where we belong."

Squeezed against him in the elevator, her lunchtime garlic breath diluted by the antiseptic smells of nurses and patients, she said gently, her harelip barely moving, "I know I said last time would be the last time, but . . . your combat wounds . . . my dad, when I was a little girl . . . I'm going to pretend that I found you upstairs, where you're supposed to be, but this time will be the last time, the very last time, and this time, this time, I'm going to have to insist that you promise"—Juke's mother's bruised lips leaving glistening snail trails of blood across Juke's contrite father's bowed, black-haired head, Juke's mother begging again and again that Juke's father would quit drinking, quit slapping her, quit shooting at long-dead German soldiers, his bullets just missing his children—Juke's father promising again and again and slapping again and again and shooting again and again and collapsing into unconsciousness again and again and again, and again awakening, begging to be forgiven, and promising again and again.

"Promise me, Juke."

"I can't—" can't lie—can't—"promise."

A kind person, the harelipped head nurse, her kindness her beauty, he'd finally realized—her kindness her beauty.

New white had covered the dead brown grass, from which, this morning—mourning—old snow had been mounded to form a snow-man and woman, now standing side by side, their shapes white against white, faint in evening's dwindling light.

"This goddamned snow," the man old enough to have been Juke's father had said this morning—mourning—stamping white powder from black rubber before going through the steam-curtained Radiation Lab door, which Juke had held open. The old soldier had come to be treated for cancer, begun when nuclear-test commanders had used World War Two combat veterans—as Nazi doctors had used Jews—as nuclear-experiment guinea pigs.

Going downhill started little snow slides, new dry snow sliding over frozen snow.

"Not white enough for you, am I? Just another goddamned Indian, same as you, and half nigger besides. Look at me."

"I'm driving. This snow and ice. I'm driving."

"Look at me, you damned, jealous redskin, you look at me."

At the party, Alita had worn an almost amber dress, just a little lighter than her complexion, and the dress was loose and moved as her body swayed, arched, and flung about in dance after dance—her skin almost pale where it stretched over delicate collarbones.

"Your girlfriend in the fucking loony bin. A Miss America, I hear—one a them be-I-you tease queens, as pale as the goddamned snow, wasn't she? That's what she was to you, wasn't she? A fucking snow-woman, patted together out of snow-white advertising paper. A Indniun high school boy's wet dream, wasn't she? Still is, isn't she—in your poor fucked-up brain. Never much in common, you two, no overabundance of intelligence and no love of literature or history or philosophy in her, no hate for the greed that's destroying our planet, no passion for justice, not like us, but a goddess, wasn't she? your goddamned so-called fiancée, who is now a goddamned snow-white vegetable, a goddamned cauliflower, made so in consequence of unmaking an unintended, unwanted foetus.

"'My fault, my buddies, my Mary,' you all the time telling me, and your mom, just like my own mom, self-sacrificing and loving, but too weak to stand up for herself and too weak to stand up for her children. Your parents, my parents, they are dead. Your buddies. Dead. Your Mary, she's the same as dead. I'm sorry, Juke, but me, I'm alive. As long as we stay here, I'll be waiting on tables and you'll be sweeping floors—can't use our education to help us make a decent living someplace else—maybe have kids of our own. How do you think I feel? Hell! Heh-ell! We're through. And the hell of it is, I love you."

Alita would be gone.

"Ain't gonna be no Scarface Indian's nigger no more," she had said, all African American again, abandoning her Indian people as she was abandoning him.

She was lovely. She knew it. Eyes told her. Words. Hands. Sure. Hell. Certainly. Half a dozen paintings of her told her. Even Scarface Juke had told her—had tried to.

Snow was gusting down from the dark pines, from the wings of sparrows settling for the night.

Alita, I love—Mary. The snow gusting against dark pines, and the scurrying mouse sounds of snow blown over snow. Mary. His hands putting the brush to Mary's blond hair, under the familiar, tangled hair, inside the tangled brain, maybe dreams, maybe memories of him, of life as it used to be, maybe nothing—the nurses, the pretty one and the old one, looking elsewhere—the least insane of the other patients looking elsewhere—away from the pitiful, loathsome pieces of human love moving slowly in the visiting hour in the white light.

Sunset exploded, red, through clouds and spread over the frozen glaze of snow.

Machine-gun bullets ripping rice plants around him, he was running—trying to run—through mud, and his buddies were already climbing into the slowly moving truck when the helicopter's rocket exploded. Crawling away from flames, through muck, which had damned near drowned him, he had saved himself, saved what was left of himself, saved somebody—somebody's son, somebody's brother, somebody's buddy, somebody's lover, and maybe, some day, somebody's father—somebody. A miracle.

The miracle of human reproduction, of mass production, of modern weaponry—the American heat-seeking rocket finding the heat of a straining American truck engine.

Washed clean by snow, melted by friction, splashed onto rubber, the father's status-symbol car's big black tire rolled over the little son's abdomen, white under the red snowsuit—and not even a broken bone, only bruises—a miracle—soft snow absorbing—the steel of the heavy-duty army truck and the bodies—so many bodies—absorbing the rocket explosion—the rice-paddy muck quelling flames—a miracle— Juke Dark Cloud, survivor of an Indian necktie, a loop of natal cord, noosed around the neck at birth, a survivor of Indian wars in the genes, a not-quite-vanished Vanishing American—a survivor of war in the family, his drunken father's war—a survivor of his own war, and the only survivor of a misdirected American rocket—a miracle.

Tiny with distance, a woman, a stranger, emerged from a bridal arch of snow-bowed bushes and, as she'd done at the end of every workday, continued walking, slowly, gracefully, crossing the frozen river.

I love you Alita Mary Father Mother God in the flutters from branch to branch above the path. Love. A miracle. And kindness. Kindness a beauty. A harelipped woman a beauty. Her letter recommending him to future employers no masterpiece of literature but an expression of kindness, a gift of beauty.

The cloud of the stranger woman's breath rose from her mouth into cold air. A red scarf was at her throat, and sundown over snow spread red like blood thinned by rice-paddy water—by water washing the operating table—Mary—Never wanted—Mother, Father, God—Mary—this baby.

The stranger woman murmured, as always, "Hi," that American compression of, "How are you?" and he—How am I? How the hell am I?—answered her smile and nodded, as always, and said, "Hi," and she vanished, as always, pale face, red lips, red scarf, black coat all hidden by pines, dark against snow, red of her scarf blazing on the horizon before him, beyond him, warming the December river to sigh open to receive him as he crossed—the river to receive him and give him peace—or nothing, nothing, nothing.

Moving his black rubber boot soles carefully up the slippery white bank, as always, he saw a light—but he knew he might have forgotten to turn it off this morning.

Stamping snow from black rubber—big black tire squashing—little lungs breathing ozone-eating auto-exhaust—a miracle—Mary Jesus father son and holy—the old World War Two survivor, American nuclear holocaust victim, stamping snow from boots—stomping the death that was in the snow—stomping the ingratitude, the hypocrisy, the injustice, the government, the nuclear scientists, the army—and pathetically grateful for a small, ordinary human kindness, a young man's holding open a heavy door.

"Juke."

"I quit my job."

"Juke, you bastard; you weren't even worried I wouldn't be here. You ain't so out of it as you let on."

"I love you, Alita."

"You mean it?"

"I don't know."

"You don't—? Juke. Juke. You study too much. You think too much. And you don't even know if you mean it when you say you love me. You're cold. You know that much anyway, don't you, you damned fool? I made coffee. Take off your boots. Come in, for Christ's sake, come on in. You quit your job? You'll have to leave here now, like the veterans counselor's been telling you, like I've been asking you. You'll have to."

"Yes."

"You will? You really will? What about your fiancée? What about Mary?"

Her hand will move, searching for her hairbrush or for a pretty blue-black fly. She'll touch her hair, her slender hand making a delicate shade in that blazing halo, evoking a vanished beauty, a vanished life.

"A miracle. A miracle that this man is alive."

"Leave here? I will. I really will."

# PART FOUR

# TERRORISM AND TERRORIZED

# Fractures, a Class Reunion

In his fifty-four years on earth, Gar Eastridge's right leg had been fractured twice: when he'd run from police on last spring's last ice while protesting U.S. torture of prisoners in Iraq, and thirty-five years back, when he had been shot by a high school classmate.

The first fracture had kept him out of combat until the Vietnam War was nearly over. The second had kept him home from teaching and let him work on poems, which would, he hoped, offer his oil-squandering, world-plundering nation something of his Cherokee forebears' reverence for nature. His book was near its publication date, and intent on making the final version as good as possible, he took it for granted that he'd miss, as usual, his high school class reunion.

"You should see what the years have made of friends, and enemies, in the town where you were born," his wife urged. She had arranged hundreds of her new novel's pages on floors, and Gar was self-pityingly ready to suspect that she found her limping husband in the way. "Unless," she said, "you're afraid to go."

Afraid? Willing to risk dying to win his talented, Scandinavian-eyed classmate, he'd bested two more sensible rivals by climbing a high river bank and diving, through calm, sunny surface, into turbulent depths. Past trout arcing like tracer bullets, body jolted by his plunge, he'd swum desperately—as he'd once flown a plane, so overloaded with wounded and dead it could barely clear jungle at the end of an airstrip—and, scarred right knee and smooth left equally bloodied by streambed gravel, he'd scrabbled ashore, while the woman he loved had cheered and his rivals had grudgingly applauded. A husband who needed to prove that his boyhood could not threaten his manhood, Gar let hands other than his own fly him over mountains, through whose snows Lewis and Clark and Sacajawea had slogged. Then, after checking into a motel where, eighteen, he'd taken a girl he'd hoped to marry, he drove his rental car past the small rental house he'd known as home. At his parents' graves, he prayed, wept, and left roses to replace wilted poppies, with which the American Legion once each year honored his "redskin" war hero dad and his Legion Auxiliary "half-breed" mom.

Gar prayed at the grave of Lance Higgins, whose killings were not celebrated by flag and blossoms. In well-intentioned, bumbling youth, Gar had tried to change Lance's life, but Lance had changed Gar's life, instead.

Passing the baseball field, on which he'd won brief glory, Gar reached the high school, whose claim to TV fame was being called what many Indian towns and Pioneer towns had been called—what many Vietnamese villages had been called—"Site of Massacre."

On red brick Roman-temple columns, imitation-gold plaques bore the names of former students and the words: "They gave their lives for their country." The Indian Wars, the Civil War, World Wars One and Two, the Korean War, the war in which Westward Ho had been halted by Ho Chi Minh, and the ongoing war for Arab oil—and still there was room for more plaques, more names, including, Gar feared, the names of his three sons.

Somewhere in the shadowy corridor ahead were the names of those whose lives had not been "given" but "taken"—taken by a boy whose insanity had not been the mass insanity of a nation at war, but the insanity of an outraged individual intent on revenge.

Joyous class-reunion noise guided Gar to the auditorium, where, thirty-six years back, four years of short-skirted, cartwheeling cheer-leaders and pep-rally chants had ended with a patriotic graduation speech and rifle shots.

After dinner, having firmly mentioned his wife and three sons to correct alcohol-inspired insinuations about his friendship with Lance Higgins, Gar buddied up around beer with men whose time in Vietnam had been longer, bloodier, and more heroic than his own. When his fellow veterans of a lost war had finished their communal griping about fighting "communist gooks" and then having to settle for politicians' "strategic withdrawal," the baseball team's catcher, now a life-insurance salesman, tried to flatter Gar by mentioning his only claim to fame other than having been interviewed on television as Lance Higgins's only friend. "You was hailed as 'a Cornbelt Carlile Indian,'" he recalled, "and you was scouted by the Cleveland Indians."

"Atlanta Braves," an outfielder, whose home runs had been overshadowed by Gar's no-hit pitching, angrily corrected. He and the catcher had loved the town's most sought-after girl, who'd married neither. Her fertility-goddess figure, altered by countless calories, mocked the beautiful confusions of youth, but her movie-starlet prettiness blossomed, through thirty-five years, in the jilted rivals' dislike of each other.

After Gar concurred that Atlanta Braves was correct, his home-run-hitting former competitor for local headlines generously, or smugly, offered, "Still got your limp, I see. Too bad you got shot."

"Yeah! That goddamned queer Lance Higgins!" Gar's one-time catcher one-upped his foe. Then, remembering Gar's children, he resumed his insurance pitch. When Gar said that he was insured through the state college where he taught, his one-time catcher muttered, "Socialism," and threw back a final defiance at his love rival: "A cornbelt Carlile Indian, he was hailed as a Cornbelt Carlile, Indian," before seeking better sales prospects and "something stronger than beer."

Answering a salary-comparison question elicited "not half what you'd of got in the big leagues," and there was disappointment that Gar hadn't at least become a pitching coach.

"I heard that Lance Higgins's big-brained, little-titted sister got one of them foreign scientific prizes," somebody said, his snicker popping the bubbles of yet another beer, and Gar knew that mention of his poetry awards would have stereotyped him as as fruity as versifiers in TV sitcoms—as as queer as Lance Higgins.

Lance. A mother who considered herself the Midwest equivalent of English nobility had cursed her son with an ancestral appellation that high school boys had found laughable. She had further cursed him with her own rose-blossom, rose-thorn beauty, which his sister might have envied.

"Queer, cocksucker, fruit," male classmates had mocked Lance—too young to acknowledge their own normal bisexuality, Gar thought, and remembered that too young to acknowledge his own normal bisexuality, he had simply believed that less-bright classmates had envied his and Lance's shared intelligence. The son of a railroad worker, Gar had welcomed the friendship of a guy whose family was, by local standards, rich. Lance's banker father drove a big black Lincoln and aided or ended politicians' careers. Lance's mother might or might not be the descendant of English nobility, as she claimed, but she ruled the school board and the school. Since Lance had chosen Gar, she decided that Gar was the "noble savage" her ancestors had praised, and she professed gratitude for Gar's influencing her son to become "more manly," able to hunt in "the Great Out of Doors" and to kill wild game for gourmet dinners, which she served to her husband's political allies.

Gar taught Lance to hunt deer by thinking as they thought—of where to find water and food, and where to hide. He taught Lance to say a prayer for deer, *Kawa*, whose flesh had fed the flesh of Gar's Cherokee people centuries before invasion.

Gar tried teaching Lance baseball, but "Why waste time on sports?" was Lance's opinion of the one skill that made Gar a part of his community, and when an Atlanta Braves' scout came to watch

Gar's third no-hit victory, Lance was the only kid who did not attend a special rally held in Gar's honor.

Lance had already been admitted to the school from which his father had graduated, Yale—Gar to the State University of Iowa, in Iowa City, Iowa. Lance had his parents' money. Gar had a baseball scholarship, but wouldn't need it if he won an Atlanta Braves contract. No longer scorned as a "redskin," he'd get a chance to win celebrity at America's national game, and he'd be able to pay his own university tuition each winter. He would study and learn to survive, not just as himself but as part of his bloodline. All creatures adapted to survive. That was living in harmony with nature, and Gar thought that he would be in harmony with nature, though he'd be throwing baseballs past batters instead of throwing rocks to hunt rabbits.

"You've left the Spirit Medicine Path you told me to follow," Lance protested. "My IQ is almost as high as my sister's, and yours is almost as high as mine. You're selling out your chance to be your best self."

Years later, his sister told Gar that the sons of some of her father's Yale friends had welcomed Lance to his admission interviews on campus, but then had involved him in something that had left Lance shaken, and had caused Lance's father to phone the local draft board—probably hoping that the military might make his son more manly. Lance lost his hope of surviving high school and getting an education among intellectual equals, who'd value him for what he valued in himself.

"My pretentious, snob mother could never face reality," Lance's sister said, "but I should have persuaded Dad to get my brother psychiatric help."

When Gar mumbled, "I should have been a better friend," Lance's sister said, in gratitude or in condemnation, what the television man had said: "You were his only friend."

Gathering to march and receive diplomas, boys made predictable teasing insinuations about Lance's oversize graduation robe's long skirts, not knowing that beneath quiet toleration of contempt, a rebellion as violent as Colonial America's war for equality would explode.

At the start of some politician's patriotic speech, Lance emerged among shadows of the auditorium's balcony.

As unable as Lance's middle-class mother to face truth, and locked into years of student habit, all of the graduating class stayed in their seats while the first shot echoed like TV news' automatic-weapons fire—but the graduation-ceremony speaker finally slowly sagging into a crimson puddle widening around his podium, everyone jumped up, as if to give a standing ovation. The graduating students' black-robed rows were the target presented to colonists imitating redskins in ambushing redcoats, who'd been ranked, with Age of Reason precision, to make muskets' firepower greater.

Rifle propped on balcony railing—gold-tasseled, flat hat cocked back—Lance's mad eyes found Gar, and unable to move, wedged between a boy on one side, a girl on the other, Gar began chanting, "Waya, Kawa, Tsi-skwa, Wadi, Sahani, Gilha, Gat-uh-geh-wi." The clan names that his parents had taught him, what TV would mistakenly praise as "a self-sacrificing effort to distract the gunman."

Hearing Gar's prayer that he might join his people after death, Lance swung his rifle back like a baseball bat cocked to swing. Moving one hand, he made the sign of the cross, ending it by thumbing his nose. Then, true to the religion he'd mocked, he forgave Gar's having failed to help him defy classmates' cruel jibes. Returning, as he might have thought, good for bad, he aimed between frantically dodging bodies.

Lance's bullet did what gun designers had intended a bullet to do. Gar would never again rear back on his right leg, lengthen his body and right arm to the utmost, then hurl what sportswriters called his "rocket-missile fast ball" past batters' bats. Lance ended Gar's—and the community's—hope of Big League baseball fame. Gar was just an Indian again, one who would never pitch for the Atlanta Braves.

Sinking into his seat—a spectator now, mesmerized by horror, numb to pain though in danger of bleeding to death—Gar heard Lance screaming as if quarterbacking football plays. "Queer!"—he shot the baseball-team captain, his worst tormentor—"Fruit!"—a mild bachelor teacher, for whom he had possibly felt unrequited love—"Cunt!"—the girl who'd deserved the class valedictorian award, which Lance's mother had had bestowed on Lance—"Cocksucker!"—the yearbook caption writer, who'd penned "Tonto, our Noble Savage" under Gar's picture, and under Lance's, "our local nobleman"—"Sissy!"—a sensitive boy who'd tried to prove his manhood by teasing Lance about the skirts of his robe—"Pussy!"—the girl Gar had, in youth's beautiful confusion of lust with love, hoped to marry.

Gar was, TV would say, "lucky"; but his "luck" had been Lance's good eyesight and steady aim. "Christ!" When Lance had shot to kill, he had killed, his final victim himself. The fractured leg delayed Gar's training for war—his time in it only a few flights, to bring home some American wounded, some American dead.

Those killed in battle and those killed by a "misfit fellow student" were buried in the same graveyard—where Gar would be buried, someday, beside his hardworking, self-sacrificing parents. Both of Lance Higgins's grandfathers had been officers in The Great War, The War to End All Wars, and their family gravestones were imposing. Lance's politically powerful World War Two–officer father and his politically adroit mother had overridden community protest and buried their only son in the space for which they'd paid.

"You were right. I was afraid to face the past," fifty-four-year-old Gar confessed, and his fifty-six-year-old wife replied, "Who isn't!"

Back at his desk, working on his collection of poems, Gar wrote Lance's sister that he'd placed flowers on her family's graves, and he also gave her belated congratulations. While watching news of smart bombs, civilian casualties, torture interrogation, and suicide bombers, in the struggle to control Arab oil, he had seen her gaunt face, as lined and wrinkled as his own but as radiant as that of a little birthday girl, her latest scientific discovery reportedly preventing one of the human race's afflictions forever.

# The Indian Who Bombed Berlin

"Little guys like you are always scared of big guys like me," my pilot told the last inch of beer between peace and having to risk being stomped by hobnailed boots while trying for another pint at the jostling bar.

We were celebrating winning World War Two and not getting killed, and he knew as much as I did about fear. Twice, he'd aborted missions over heavily defended primary targets and had ordered me to dump our bombloads on secondary targets. Though bigger than any of the forty or so British soldiers in the pub nearest our airbase, he was one of only two "overpaid, oversexed, and over here, bloody Yanks." Downgraded from rescuing hero to enviously resented foreigner, he was dumping his anger on a safe target—"Tonto," his "Red Nigger" bombardier, me.

To keep my self-respect, I postured like generations of Davids threatened by generations of Goliaths and quoted my five foot eight father: "The bigger they come the harder they fall." An Indian married to a white, Dad had more than once had to make his boast good. I was dark enough to have heard myself called "Wog" when in the company of English women, but, five foot six and not brave enough to follow Dad's warrior example, I had ignored the insult.

"Actually, little guys have nothing to be scared about," my pilot told his empty mug; then, when I made no move to get refills, he told me, "Big guys won't usually beat up little guys. But, sure's hell, we can if we want to."

It was a truth that Ethiopia, Albania, Czechoslovakia, Poland, Holland, Belgium, Denmark, Norway, Finland, Yugoslavia, Greece, and others had recently rediscovered—a truth that enormous allied armies had just taught Germany.

"The only war won is a war not fought," I'd read, and my victory was persuading two women, as young and as joyous as my pilot and me, to share my bottle of officers-ration gin and a beautiful confusion of love and lust in their nearby flat.

Nineteen, sexually unashamed, and—thanks to luck and to colonization of rubber-producing nations—undiseased, I returned from the most colossal historic event of my time, began to feel the shallowness of womanizing, and—after months of dating and then living together—married a college classmate.

When our daughter was grown and in college, I won a fellowship, "To Further," my award stipulated, "International Understanding," by teaching Stage and Screen courses to German university students, who were admirably fluent in English.

Having bombed puzzle patterns of tiny city blocks glimpsed through clouds, and through clouds of smoke, I was shocked—as my older brother, a veteran of ground war, had said I would be—by the devastation of cathedrals and homes, not only in big prime target cities but in small secondary targets, like the ones on which my pilot had twice ordered me to salvo our bombs. Troubled, as I'd not been when staring at maps and bomb-sight, I only acknowledged, if asked, having bombed one city, the center of Hitler's government—an evasion that prompted a Drama Department colleague, a former British bomber pilot, to sneer a mocking warrior name, "The Indian Who Bombed Berlin."

I was teaching Writing for Stage and Screen, a class he had taught for years. He had written plays produced on London stages, while my main qualification was having had two plays produced—one off Broadway, and one so far off Broadway its American Southeastern Indian characters were portrayed by actors speaking in West Coast Canadian accents. The Englishman felt that my teaching his class, even for a year, was an injustice. It was a small injustice, perhaps, compared to that which had been inflicted on professors, students, and their pursuit of truth in Nazi Germany—and in increasingly right-wing America—and compared to injustices then being inflicted in Stalinist Russia, East Germany, and in many nations ruled by religious tyrants. It was small compared to the injustice inflicted on my Native American people. Still, injustice was injustice.

To my British colleague, I was over here, overpaid, and underqualified, and his dislike grew when he heard my televised lecture mentioning England's having enslaved Native Americans, Africans, and Asians. I also mentioned migrant laborers, whom European nations and the U.S. had recruited, then consigned to poverty as domestic human reproduction caught up with the job needs of industrial production. I spoke of Indians whom starvation had driven to hopeless rebellion, and expressed doubt that Hitler could have gained power had not Germans been suffering from enemy-imposed hunger.

"In our nuclear age," I concluded, "war is the societal equivalent of suicide."

My British colleague renewed redcoat-redskin hostilities, declaring, "Eight years I've taught here and haven't had to kiss Hitler's dead arse to do it. It wouldn't be me, but someone should let Washington know about their redskin wog's subversive blather."

His hatred of "wogs" reportedly included his former wife's having had a child by a black American soldier, and it included his Turkish students, who'd been made increasingly "uppity" by having seen what "nigger mobs" had recently won in the U.S.A.

I got on well with German students, most of them strongly egalitarian, and due to my wog complexion and to my being from a former British colony, where we wogs had gained some constitutional rights, I got on especially well with the sons and daughters of Turkish workers, who'd been recruited for jobs in Germany but not been given German citizenship.

Walking to my class, one hot midday, I found my route blocked by thousands of dark-skinned demonstrators, who were marching, under Turkish and a number of other Near East and Middle East banners, to present the city government with a demand for social justice. Caught between the river and a fortress wall, whose stones had echoed to the footbeats of Roman invaders, I was just one among dozens of spectators, but my British colleague, who was standing nearby, shouted something in fluent German to a group whose signs called for Holy War.

Pulled into the march, I thought the group wanted another dark-skinned man to add to their numbers, and I tried to protest, in my not-very-fluent German, that I would soon be due to teach a class.

"Murderer! Satan American! Murderer!" a tall man shouted and slapped my jaw. I automatically struck back, hitting him or hitting someone else crowded around me in the line of march. My arms were seized, and I was pummeled, as my British colleague had been after parachuting into a city he'd just bombed.

The bigger the gang, the greater the pain they can inflict, I'd learned in America's schoolyards—and, my Cherokee warrior father's courage only going to incite more blows, I tried cowardly submission. It hadn't worked for my outnumbered Indian forebears, and it didn't work for me.

My hair grabbed from behind and my face jerked up to be visible on a TV camera, positioned high above the jostling marchers, I was struck hard on the back of the head. Afraid I'd lose consciousness, go down, and be kicked or trampled to death by hundreds of feet, with my wife watching the midday news, I wrenched free from hands holding my arms, but was immediately seized by other hands.

Staring through plastic riot shields, police probably only saw me as part of a flow of dark-skinned people, legally marching on designated streets to disrupt no traffic. When the TV crew and the police protecting their truck were behind us, someone yelled, "Throw him in the river!" and, everything shouted loud enough becoming a slogan, dozens chanted, "In, in, throw him in!"

My father had tried to teach me to swim, but had only succeeded in teaching me to be afraid of water. Dragged onto a bridge, which I and other bombardiers had failed to destroy, I struggled, but hands gripped my arms tighter. My captors were as small as myself, but they were numerous, they were younger, and they were strong. I walked in step with the two who held my arms, hoping they'd forget the threat that I should be drowned.

We were halfway across the bridge. The incentive of striking boast-worthy blows against Satanic America in front of TV cameras gone, punching had become perfunctory cuffing, but there'd be renewed energy once we'd reached more TV crews, just beyond this bridge.

I tried the war whoop, with which I'd once driven off a pack of dogs before they could do more than slash a friend's child's legs. This time, I didn't even have my tennis racket as a weapon, but the war whoop producing expectant silence, I shouted, with memories of a few racists in wartime London, "WOGS OF THE WORLD UNITE!"

That evoked answering shouts from marchers outside the group that had grabbed me, "Unite! Unite! Unite!" and hoping to be released to join in protest, I chanted with hundreds of other dark-skinned people, "Unite! Unite! Unite!"

Trained as an actor, and schooled to be whatever white culture required I be, I tried to sound like the other marchers, but I was not the Holy War group's casting director, nor was I allowed to create the script. Just before we got to the far end of the bridge, four men grabbed my ankles and wrists, and swung my vainly struggling body back and forth. Then I was for the second time in my life flying above the bridge—this time not thousands of feet above, but just enough to clear the low stone railing.

As I fell, one brown face above me became my father's face, its expression that of concern, and I was six again, about to sink or swim.

I sank, sun-glow breath-bubbles bursting—sank until my feet plunged into mud. Choking on water and on oil leaked from boats, I frantically thrashed my arms, straightened my back, and found my head and shoulders in air.

Drowning a small, unimportant American—and going to prison—had not been the plan. Having terrified and humiliated a supposed enemy, my captors were probably, by now, far along the line of march. Brown faces staring over the bridge railing, ten feet above my staring, brown face, were as sympathetic as the pale faces of men and women, staring over the rails of a floating restaurant, anchored a few feet away.

No one wanted to extend a hand and risk ruining his good clothes, but by holding onto the gangplank, I was able to stumble ashore and walk, water squishing inside shoes, over cobblestones put into place centuries back. In a classroom building that had housed American occupation troops, I tried to honor the terms of my grant, and "Further International Understanding," by lecturing, barefoot, to students as young as I had been when I'd bombed not only Berlin, but many other cities.

Most of my life I've taught in universities, three times in Germany. And by now, two generations after two atomic implosions, my father's warrior boast, "The bigger they come the harder they fall," means the U.S. defeat in Vietnam—means the USSR's defeat in Afghanistan—and means that, in our nuclear age, bigger nations are only bigger targets.

"Murderer!"

Having heard the truth made my own international understanding more clear. I can't restore men's, women's, and children's lives, but I can try to make my own life, and those of others, somewhat better—can still try to change injustice to justice, still try to keep our species' suicidal tantrums from rendering us all extinct.

# Between Buses, Between Wars

The first to descend our local bus's steps to wait, beside a highway, for an interstate bus, a big battle-ribboned, blond soldier seized bare upper arms and lifted down a pretty, dark-skinned woman, who was protesting, "No, no," and pressing a college-bookstore bag against her wind-rippled red skirt.

My gray hair and wedding band probably reassuring, the woman sat beside me on the only bench and, despite intense desert sunlight, began to read.

"I'll be right back," the young soldier insisted; but before he could collect his duffel bag, a dark, middle-aged man claimed the space next to the young woman.

The soldier clenched his fists. Then, shaking his head and smiling, he stepped sideways in front of the woman and bowed as if to read the cover of her book, whose sun-reflecting pages made her slender throat glow.

"Where my parents' big goddamned ranch is, the Indians there they all got shit for brains," the soldier said. "But you're a Indian, and you're studying American history. Good for you. Me, I'm making history. I freed Afghanistan. Now, I'm off to another godforsaken terrorist place."

"Oh, that's too bad," not the response he wanted, he said, "No! That's *duty*. Just like your book there is telling you. Or ought to be telling you, if it ain't. Our training officers, they told us. Our forefathers took civilization across the Atlantic and all the way to the Pacific. It was Manifest Destiny then, it's Manifest Destiny now, and it'll be Manifest Destiny forever! There's no way we're going to let foreigners keep us from getting our oil." Still standing over the Indian woman, but half turned toward the Indian man, he demanded, "If you got muscles and balls, you got to use 'em or lose 'em. Right, Chief?"

Black eyes downcast, the Indian's face was not a noble movie chief's face. His expression was submissive, his "Yo, Sarge," mumbled.

"Age you are and way you said, 'Sarge,' must be you got the shakes, or whatever's wrong with you, while you was trying to free Vietnam. That's where my daddy's daddy, he got sent."

The Indian stared out across the miles of high desert sagebrush, to a snowy mountain horizon and up at blurry white trails of jetliners or bombers, his skinny body trembling.

"Coward!" the sergeant muttered in Japanese, then, my pale face showing disapproval, said, "Yes, Sir, I had some good times in Japan. And you, old man, you understand gook talk?"

"Just English," I could truthfully say, need for my textbook Japanese having ended when World War Two ended.

"Just English? You trying to lump English in with gook talk? You got a damned strange accent for being out here in cowboy country. Where you from?"

"Another former British colony, Canada, but I've taught for thirty years in universities here in the States, and your accent is strange to me. Where are you from?"

"Even my parents' neighbors ask me," he laughed. "I've been gone so long nobody can tell I'm from right here. God's country. Eastern Oregon. Professor, huh? Maybe you know what them sand niggers talk where they're causing this latest brouhaha."

"Arabic," I guessed, thinking, Money—oil money—is what really talks.

"Canada didn't fight loose from England when we did, did they? Did they ever fight?"

"Both World Wars." My father had been conscripted for the "War to End All Wars," and I'd volunteered for World War Two, age eighteen—to save democracy, I'd thought. "Canada helped U.S. draft dodgers get out of fighting in Vietnam," the young American told me. "Not my grandaddy. And not my grandaddy's grandson neither. Germs, gas—whatever's next, I won't be no coward. Not like some." He glanced scornfully at the Indian man, whose trembling hands were fumbling with the zipper of a backpack. Then, again muttering his Japanese insult, he seized the young woman's shirt front and told her, "My daddy he has a weak heart, and he never got drafted to do no fighting in no wars, but my daddy's daddy, he sacrificed his life for our country in Vietnam. I spit on wimps who stayed out of the army by going to Canada or by going to schools like your Lane"—staring at stenciled letters he'd twisted tight across her breasts—"Community College."

Shouting, "Stop it!" the young woman sprang to her feet, pivoted, and got free.

The soldier's big fingers convulsing, as if to seize and choke, I felt as I'd felt when I'd translated sobbed complaints of rape for shrugging military police, and I did not know if I should try to protect the woman, with or without the trembling Indian man's help, or if I should run as fast as my elderly legs would take me and hope to, sooner or later, flag down a driver, who might go for police.

The Indian man groping inside his backpack, I glimpsed, tucked among rolled socks and underwear, a knife—only a slender, fish-fileting knife, but a knife.

Arrogantly glancing at the Indian man and me, then staring at the few inches of thighs bare below the young woman's red skirt, the big soldier said, "I'll show you what it takes to be a real man." Unfastening the belt of his uniform pants, he pulled free the tails of his battle-ribboned shirt and began unbuttoning.

I gripped my briefcase, heavy with books, to serve as a weapon or a shield, rose and moved onto the secure footing of the highway, prepared to fight or to flee. "You want to know what it means to be an American soldier?"

The young man spread his shirt against the wind, displaying a pink scar that curved from navel to blond-hair-fringed nipple, its stitch marks flared, like the legs of a centipede. "Bayonet, you'd think," he said, "but, no, it was a bullet that tore *across* me instead of *into* me's the only reason I'm alive and the Taliban who aimed up out of his foxhole and shot me he ain't!"

Black eyes fixed on the blond soldier, the Indian man said something, his language probably once the only one spoken in that sparsely populated part of the American West. Then, there had been an invasion, followed by all that conquest empowers the conqueror to enjoy—massacre, torture, rape. The young Indian woman's complexion was lighter than that of the middle-aged Indian man, but apparently she spoke the same language, because whatever he'd said caused her to sit down and place one slender finger in her book.

"My kinsman would not say it and would not have others say it," she told the blond soldier, "but TV has said it, and I will say it. He was a hero—a hero who risked his life for others—and he has suffered as you have suffered. I need to study for exams, but he tells me that you need to talk. I will listen."

"No," the young soldier mumbled, "You gotta do what you gotta do. I gotta do what I gotta do. That's just the way it is." He sank onto the end of our bench and began buttoning his shirt, his battle ribbons as bright as flag stripes, or rows of cemetery petals, in the desert sun.